# MILO
## The Legend

**PRESS**

14172 E Carlson Rd. • Brule, WI 54820
(218) 391-3070 • www.savpress.com

# MILO
## The Legend

David L. Waldbillig

*David L. Waldbillig*

# DEDICATION

To the horse and to everyone who loves horses.

# ACKNOWLEDGMENTS

Thank you to my cousin, Ms. Paula Musetta, for the the inspiration to continue with this book and for the typing; Marion Schmidt, Patty Palm, and Theresa Shanoff, also cousins, for their support; Lisa Manty for continued inquiries about the progress while I visited the supermarket; Pauline Campbell for additional typing;  Lisa Gebhart, who exposed me to her team of horses; and Michael Savage and Debra Zime for the publishing of this book.

# TABLE OF CONTENTS

## CHAPTER 1 | **MILO IS BORN**

Milo came from a sparkling cloud of Mist. He was pink in color. His eyes were dark brown. He almost looked mystical. He was small and timid. The horse fairies flew around him, laughing. They said, "Milo, do not be afraid."

It was the first time Milo heard his name. He said, "Milo. Milo is my name?"

"Yes," the fairies said. "You are a very special horse. Milo, you will never get old, and we will be your guardians forever!"

Milo said, "Forever? You mean I'll live FOREVER?"

"Holy Cow," Milo said, "this is really cool!"

The horse fairies said, "Milo, how did you know there was a Holy Cow?"

Milo said, "I didn't know there was a Holy Cow. The words just came out. Besides, what IS a Holy Cow?"

The horse fairies laughed and said, "Oh, Milo, you have so much to learn."

Milo said, "Oh, please, teach me everything you know."

The fairies said, "EVERYTHING?"

Milo said, "Everything!"

The fairies said, "Later, Milo. We have a job to do. We have to color you."

"Color me?" Milo said, "But I thought I was going to be pink?"

"Oh no, Milo. We will paint you, and you will be a masterpiece!"

Milo said, "A masterpiece! I wonder what a masterpiece is?"

The fairies said, "Oh, Milo, you just wait and see!"

Milo said, "Okay…but I hope it's something special!"

The fairies said, "Oh, Milo, we have never failed. We are the BEST of the BEST! We have painted all the horses in the world and in this dimension."

"The World." That was the second time they had said that word! *I wonder what they mean? The World. The Dimension….*

The fairies said, "Oh Milo, be patient. You have so much to learn. Now hold still!"

The fairies flew around looking like little brown swirls in the air.

When Milo was born, the horse fairies did not know what color he should be.
So they painted Milo tan and white, as you can plainly see.
They stood back and looked at him and laughed with glee.
They said, "Oh, we're not finished. You just wait and see."
They got out their black brushes and began to paint and sing.
They painted Milo's tail black and thought he looked so fine!
"So if we paint his mane black he will look divine!"
They looked at him and said, "There's something missing here.
Let's put a black edge on each ear."
The horse fairies said, "There is one more thing to do.
We must paint his nose black too.
Yes, Milo is a masterpiece that you don't often see!"

When they painted Milo's nose black, they were very careful. They hummed a song, a very quiet song. It was almost an eerie sound. Milo became very tired. He fell asleep on his feet. His brown eyes were almost closed. He dreamed he was running across a field of green grass.

"Hey, Milo! Wake up!" The fairies grabbed Milo by the ears and he awoke. That was the first time Milo ever had his ears touched and didn't like it at all!

"Please don't touch my ears," Milo said, "It makes me dizzy!"

"Oh, Milo, that's all part of being a horse."

Milo said, "But I sure don't like it!"

The fairies said, "Someday we will tell you all about the 'ear thing,' but it's time to learn how to walk."

Milo said, "Walk? What's that?"

The fairies said, "Remember in the dream, you were running?"

Milo said, "Yes."

The fairies said, "Well, Milo, you have to learn to walk before you can run."

So the horse fairies touched Milo's legs very gently. Milo's legs tingled as the fairies flew up and down on them.

Milo said, "Ohhhh! That feels so good!"

The fairies said, "Okay Milo, take a step." Milo took a step. "Wow! I moved," Milo said. "This is great!"

Milo's legs wiggled around. He took one step at a time.

Milo asked, "Wow, I wonder what it'll be like to run?"

The horse fairies said, "Don't get in a hurry." They flew up and down touching Milo's legs. Soon he was walking perfectly.

The fairies said, "All right, Milo, run!" They touched his hooves and he began to run. Faster and faster Milo ran.

Milo said, "I can't believe how fast I can run!"

The fairies said, "Oh Milo, you ain't seen nothing yet! When you get full-grown, you will be able to run like the wind."

Milo said, "Holy Cow! You mean I'll be able to run as fast as the wind can blow?"

"You got it, Milo!" The fairies said.

Milo thought back about the previous conversation with the horse fairies. They had said the word "full-grown." *I wonder what that means?*

"Hey, fairies, what do you mean by full-grown?"

The horse fairies giggled. "Oh Milo, you will become much taller and much longer. Your neck will become l-o-n-g-e-r, your head will become b-i-g-g-e-r, your legs will be l-o-n-g and you will be able to run like the wind!"

Milo said, "Holy Cow!" Milo thought for a minute. *Gee, I wonder why I keep saying "Holy Cow?" I wish the fairies would tell me about the Holy Cow.*

The horse fairies looked at Milo and they said, "Hey Milo, you look tired."

Milo said, "I am." So the horse fairies touched Milo's nose and began to hum. Milo began to fall asleep, but before he fell totally asleep, he thought of the word "hay." *I wonder what the word "hay" is....* And his eyes closed.

The horse fairies covered Milo with a *Blanket of Sparkling Mist*. They truly loved him. They sat on Milo's nose and said, "Milo is a masterpiece." And they went to sleep.

## CHAPTER 2 | **NEW THINGS**

The horse fairies awoke. They sat on Milo's nose and laughed.

"Should we wake him up? Yes!"

They removed the *Blanket of Sparkling Mist* and began to tickle Milo's ear. He awoke. He began to laugh. The fairies said, "He is laughing!"

Milo said, "Laughing?"

"Yes," the fairies said. "Doesn't it feel good?"

Milo said, "It really makes me feel happy!"

The fairies said, "Milo, you should laugh as much as you can and be as happy as you can be."

Milo said, "Oh, I love this!" He began to run and laugh. He made the fairies laugh too! The fairies caught Milo. They said, "It is time to learn to sing!"

Milo said, "Sing? What's that?"

The fairies said, "Oh Milo, you are going to love singing! Put your head back, open your mouth."

The fairies flew inside Milo's mouth. They touched his vocal chords and rubbed them with a magical dust. It was singing dust. The fairies looked at each other and said, "See how beautiful his vocal chords are? Milo will be a great singer!"

The fairies flew out of Milo's mouth. "Okay, Milo, we are finished."

Milo closed his mouth,

he coughed

and sneezed!

Milo looked at the fairies and said, "Man that was weird!"

The fairies said, "We know Milo, but now you will be able to sing!"

Milo put his head back and beautiful sounds came out of his mouth! And then Milo sang a horse song.

The fairies looked at Milo in awe, "My goodness! We have never heard such a beautiful voice!" Milo's voice echoed through the hills. His voice was divine. The fairies looked at each other and said, "Someday we will take Milo to see the Holy Cow, and he will sing for her. Milo is truly a masterpiece! Hey, Milo, stop singing!"

Milo stopped and looked at the fairies, they were crying!

"What's wrong, fairies?" Milo asked. "Why are you crying?"

The fairies said, "Tears of joy, Milo, tears of joy." The fairies dried their tears and laughed. Milo laughed too.

Milo said, "Boy, do I love happiness! It is the BEST of the BEST!"

The fairies said, "Hey Milo, it is time for you to see yourself. We will take you to Mirror Lake and you will be able to see yourself in the reflection of t he water."

Milo nodded his head and swished his tail. Milo said, "What was that? Something hit me on the butt!"

The fairies said, "That's your tail! Look behind yourself, Milo."

Milo looked back, "What's that for?" Milo began to move his tail—back and forth and up and down.

"Your tail is for keeping the bugs off you."

"BUGS?"

"Yes," the fairies replied. "In the real world there are bugs!"

Milo thought. *Bugs, World, Holy Cow, Hay, Ear Thing. These fairies are driving me nuts!*

The fairies touched Milo's ears!

Milo thought, *Please don't touch my ears!*

The fairies said, "Be careful what you think Milo, because we can read your mind." It was the first time the fairies spoke seriously. Their faces had a serious look.

Milo hung his head and said, "Oh fairies, I am so sorry."

The fairies touched Milo's shoulders. "Milo, we love you so much and now we are your guardians forever. Let's go to Mirror Lake!"

Milo started to sing. The fairies led him to Mirror Lake.

The lake was huge! It was like a piece of glass. Milo couldn't believe what he was seeing. "What is it?" Milo asked.

The fairies said, "It's water! It's the gift of life, Milo. Without water we could not exist."

"Holy Cow!" Milo said.

The fairies said, "And now, Milo, we will drink the water. The water is truly the gift of life."

They took Milo to the edge of the lake, he looked down at the water, and he saw his reflection in the water! "Holy Cow! Is that me?"

"Yes, Milo, that is what a horse looks like."

"Man! Not too bad! I like it!"

The fairies looked at each other and said, "Milo, you have good self-esteem!"

Milo didn't even hear what they said. He touched his lips to the water and began to drink. Milo thought about how wonderful the water tasted.  It made his lips , tongue, vocal chords, throat and stomach feel so good!  It was truly the gift of life!  It was the BEST of the BEST!

The horse fairies drank the water and then they began to dance across the water. They giggled and splashed water on each other, and Milo laughed at them. He felt so happy!

"Hey, Milo, come on in! The water is fine. This is a safe lake to swim in."

Milo walked into the water, "Hey fairies, can I really swim?"

"Yes, Milo, all horses know how to swim. It comes naturally."

Milo started swimming. The water felt so good on his body.

The fairies said, "You needed a bath anyway!"

Milo said, "So did you!"

The horse fairies took Milo to the top of a hill when the swim was finished. "We'll sleep here."

They touched Milo's nose and began to hum the same eerie song. Milo's eyes began to close and soon he was asleep. The fairies pulled the *Blanket of Sparkling Mist* over Milo and sat by his nostrils. The warm air from his nostrils kept them warm, and they went to sleep.

When the fairies awoke, they noticed Milo's head was much bigger. His whole body was full-grown. The fairies said, "The water from Mirror Lake has made him grow to full-size."

They laughed, "Should we wake him?"

The smallest fairy flew up and grabbed Milo's ear. "Wake up, you big old horse!"

Milo awoke. His muscles felt stiff. Milo stood up, he staggered around, he felt dizzy, and he was tall…and long…and lean! Muscles bulged from his chest. Milo was full-grown!

Milo walked down to the lake to look at himself. He looked magnificent!

The fairies flew around him singing, "Milo, you are a masterpiece!"

Milo trotted around. His muscles loosened up. He began to run.

Wind came over the hill. "Hey, Milo, do you wanna race?"

Milo said, "Yes, I would love to race you."

Wind said, "Follow me!" The race began.

Ten…twenty…thirty…forty…fifty…sixty…seventy…eighty…ninety…one hundred miles per hour! Wind blew, and Milo ran.

Milo's hooves thundered across the hills. Wind said, "That Milo can run as fast as I can blow!"

Milo could not believe what he had just done. He laughed, and the fairies gave him a big hug.

Wind said, "Goodbye," and blew away.

## CHAPTER 3 | **MILO DISCOVERS THE WORLD**

The fairies said, "Hey, Milo, come with us! We want to show you something." They walked along, smelling the air. "Wait! Stop!" the fairies said. "Milo, do you smell something?"

Milo said, "Yes! What is that?"

The fairies said, "It's horse poop."

"Horse poop?!" Milo said.

"Yes," the fairies said. "You see, Milo, in the world, horses eat hay and grass and they poop. That's how it smells."

Milo laughed, "You have got to be kidding!"

"No, Milo, we don't kid. There's got to be a portal close by." The fairies flew around sniffing the air.

"Here it is! This is the way to get into the world. Normally, there will be a hole just big enough to get your head through. Milo, we will cover the hole with the *Blanket of Sparkling Mist* . When we count to three, you stick your head through. One–two–three!"

Milo stuck his head through the hole. He couldn't believe what he saw! The fairies flew around Milo's head. "Now, Milo, we will explain what you are looking at…a red barn, a field with small trees in it, a hay pile, and three horses eating hay."

Milo said, "They look like me, but they are different colors! The small one! What's he, just a foal?"

"No, Milo, he's full-grown. He's what you call a pony. That's as big as he will get."

"Poor guy! I am glad I'm not a pony!"

The fairies said, "That red thing is a human's barn."

Milo said, "What's a human's barn?"

"Milo, give us a break. Let us explain to you what a human's barn is!"

"Okay," Milo said.

"A barn is for horses to get in out of the weather. In the world, it gets hot and cold, it rains and snows. It is their shelter. The horses in the world do not have a *Blanket of Sparkling Mist* to protect them. Milo, we want you to pull your head out of the hole now. That's enough for today."

Milo pulled his head out, and the fairies closed the hole.

"Milo, tomorrow we will tell you what a human is, but now you must rest." The fairies touched Milo's nose and began to hum. They pulled the *Blanket of Sparkling Mist* over him, and they all went to sleep.

Milo awoke the next morning. The fairies were sitting on his nostrils sleeping. He blew his nose, and the fairies flew through the air. "There," Milo said, "that's better than getting your ears pulled!"

The fairies laughed and flew back and sat on Milo's back. "Hey Milo, give us a ride!"

Milo said, "Oh no. No rides until you tell me what a human is!"

The fairies laughed. "We are not going to tell you what a human is until you sing us a song."

"Oh, okay." So Milo sang a short horse song for the fairies. They loved it!

"Okay, Milo, get ready. We'll now tell you what a human is. It is a human being. Humans are totally different than animals. You are an animal. Humans walk on two legs because that's all they have."

Milo said, "Poor things!"

"They cannot run like the wind either, Milo. They are very fragile. You must be careful around them or you could hurt them badly."

Milo looked at the fairies. "Can they sing?"

"Yes."

"Can they laugh?"

"Yes."

"Can they be happy?"

The fairies replied softly, "Yes."

"Do they love horses?"

"Some do."

"Do you think humans will like me?"

"Ohhhhhhhh, Milo, humans will love you, just like we do! That's why we brought you here; we want you to know what the world is like. Now, Milo, we have something else to tell you about humans. There are girls and there are boys."

This was really getting confusing. Milo thought, *I better quit asking questions and just go with the flow.* The fairies could hear Milo's thoughts and said, "That's right, Milo, you just better go with the flow." The fairies brushed Milo after he had finished his daily workout of trotting and galloping.

Milo said, "That feels good!"

"Yes, we've got to get you looking good, Milo, because tomorrow we will open the portal and ride you into the world." The fairies finished brushing Milo. "Well, Milo, we better get some sleep." They touched Milo's nose and they began to hum. They pulled the *Blanket of Sparkling Mist* over him. They sat on his nose and they looked at each other.

The head fairy said, "We are so lucky the Holy Cow gave us the Milo Assignment." They all agreed and went to sleep.

Milo didn't sleep much that night. He lay awake for hours! The fairies were snoring and didn't seem to be concerned. A lot of things went through Milo's mind. *What was the purpose of all this?* He could have been chosen to be just a regular horse. Why did he have to be so special? Why would he live forever? Milo finally fell asleep.

The next morning, the fairies woke Milo. They did not even touch his ears. They quietly sang a beautiful song in his ears. Milo awoke. He had never heard this song before. "What is that song?"

"Milo," the fairies said, "it's a song from the Special Place, and we are the only ones that can sing it."

Milo said, "It is beautiful! It makes me feel so good! It makes me feel full of faith. It makes me feel full of love. It makes me feel full of charity. It makes me feel full of hope."

"Yes, Milo," the fairies said, "and you will take these feelings into the world. Alright, Milo, let's find the portal." The fairies and Milo walked along, smelling the air.

"Wait!" Milo said, "I think I smell horse poop."

The fairies flew over to his nose. "Yes, it's straight ahead."

They walked for just a short distance. The head fairy said, "This is it! We have found the portal!"

The horse fairies got on Milo's back. The *Blanket of Sparkling Mist* was in front of them.

"Okay, Milo, walk slowly through the mist." And Milo walked into the world.

They walked across the field. Chassie, Breaker, and Minute Man were standing and eating hay. It was spring so there was not much grass yet. Milo walked up to them.

Breaker said, "Hi, Milo!"

Milo said, "How do you know my name?"

"My mother, Chassie told me you were coming."

Milo asked, "How did she know that?"

"Oh, she's got extrasensory perception. She always knows what's going to happen."

"Really," Milo said, "what a gift!"

"Yeah," Breaker said, "that's why she has lived so long. She's thirty-two years old."

Chassie walked over and looked at Milo. "Breaker, why do you have to tell everyone how old I am?"

Breaker said, "I'm sorry, Mom."

Chassie turned to look at Milo and said, "Hi, you came to the world to deliver faith, hope, love, and charity? It's about time! Where have you been? The world is nuts!" And Chassie started to laugh.

Milo looked at her and smiled. "It's a pleasure to meet you, Chassie."

Minute Man walked over to Milo. He said, "Hi, big shot. Wanna fight?"

"Uh, no," Milo said.

"Ahhh! You're chicken, huh?"

Milo said, "No-o-o…I'm a horse."

Minute Man said in a sing-song voice, "Chicken, chick-en! Milo's a little chicken!"

Minute Man reached out and bit Milo!

A feeling came over Milo he had never felt before. It was a feeling of rage! His lips rolled back and his teeth showed. He spun around so fast that he was a blur!

The fairies hollered, "Stop, Milo! Stop!"

Milo paused. He did not kick.

"Milo, remember you can run like the wind. Your kick would be deadly! Minute Man would not survive."

Milo's feeling of rage went away. "Oh, I'm so sorry, fairies. I'm so sorry, Minute Man."

Minute Man hung his head and said, "I am so sorry, Milo. I am sorry I antagonized you."

Milo reached out and touched Minute Man with his nose, and they became friends.

Milo looked at Breaker and said, "Come with me." Breaker and Milo walked to the little hill in the pasture. "Breaker, your mother has been a perfect horse. She has been chosen to go to the Special Place. No one knows when she will go there. But when she goes to the Special Place, she will drink milk from the Holy Cow and she will become young again."

Breaker said, "Are you sure?"

Milo said, "If you ever catch me telling a lie, you can rub a horse turd in my eye!"

Breaker laughed, and Milo laughed. Breaker knew his mother was perfect and now she would get the ultimate reward!

Milo and Breaker walked back to Minute Man and Chassie.

Milo said, "Hey, Minute Man, is it alright if I call you Pony?"

"Yes, lots of horses call me Pony. It's my nickname."

Milo looked at Pony and said, "I wonder why that name stands out to me?"

Pony walked over to Milo. "Hey Milo, I've got to tell you something."

Milo said, "What's that?"

"It's a secret! Get closer." Pony whispered, "I don't want anyone to hear."

"Ahhh! You just want to bite me!"

Pony was still whispering, "No, I don't."

"I'll tell you what, Pony. You bite me, and I'll kick your butt!"

"Well, Milo, do you know what a vampire is?"

"I sure do. They're flying blood-suckers!"

"Well, Milo, there's an old vampire that lives in the barn."

Milo was really excited, "You have gotta be kiddin'!"

"No, Milo, it's the truth! On the moonlit nights, he rides me. We have a ball! And when he rides me, I can fly!"

"Really?" Milo said, "And does he suck blood?"

"No Milo, he hasn't got any teeth! You see, when he was young, he used to fly around like a nut. One night he ran head first into the barn and knocked all his teeth out. So now he just eats bugs and hay. Uh, Milo, if you want to make him mad when you meet him, just call him 'Bugsy.'"

Milo said, "You're sure a troublemaker, Pony!" And they both laughed until tears ran down their cheeks.

Milo walked over to the balsam trees.

The fairies said, "Now we must sleep." They touched Milo's nose and his brown eyes began to close. They pulled the *Blanket of Sparkling Mist* over Milo, and they all went to sleep.

## CHAPTER 4 | **MR. COOL AND THE HORSES**

Milo and the fairies awoke. The fairies looked at Milo and said, "Hey Milo, how come you never asked us what our names were?"

Milo said, "I guess I never thought about it!"

The six fairies laughed and said, "Well Milo, we will tell you. The first fairy's name is Faith. The second fairy's name is Hope. The third fairy's name is Charity. The fourth fairy's name is Love. The fifth fairy's name is Mika, and the sixth fairy's name is Joan. Mika and Joan are Arch Fairies. Arch Fairies are super strong. They can handle everything but Mother Nature."

Just then, a pileated woodpecker came flying by. Mika and Joan flew up; they gently grabbed him by the wings, and brought him to Milo. Milo couldn't believe what he had just seen Mika and Joan do!

Milo said, "What is it?"

Mika and Joan spoke at the same time with their voices in harmony, "This is a bird Milo. This is a woodpecker!"

Milo said, "Why do you both speak at the same time?"

"The Holy Cow made us this way. If you ever see her, ask her."

Milo looked at the woodpecker and said, "You sure are beautiful!"

"Thanks Milo" the woodpecker said. "I appreciate that!"

Milo said, "What do you do?"

"Well Milo, I peck holes in dead trees and eat bugs out of them."

"Hey woodpecker, have you ever seen the vampire? He eats bugs too."

"No Milo, the vampire only comes out at night, and we always sleep at night."

Milo said, "Smart birds!"

The woodpecker said, "Well Milo, I have got some pecking to do." And he flew away.

Milo said, "Boy fairies, I sure like Mr. Woodpecker. He is a really cool guy!"

"Yes," the fairies said, "we call him Mr. Cool! Now let's go wake up the other horses. It's time for breakfast."

Milo never had eaten anything. He really doesn't have to eat or drink. The Holy Cow made him that way, but the fairies wanted him to eat to experience what it was like.

"Remember when Milo drank from Mirror Lake, how much he liked it?" the fairies asked.

So Milo ate some hay and oats. "Not bad," he said, "sure is dry though. I guess I need some water."

He took a drink out of the water pail. It wasn't as good as water from Mirror Lake. It kind of tasted like horse spit! Milo said, "I sure am glad I can do without!"

Chassie and Breaker laughed. Then Pony said, "Oh, you will get used to it after awhile."

Pony said, "Eat, eat, eat. I love to eat. I can just about eat anything!"

Milo said, "I suppose you have eaten horse poop!"

"Yeah," Pony said, "it ain't bad if it's got some oats in it."

"Man, Pony, you are making me sick!"

Pony began to sing,

"Pony is my name.
Eatin' is my game. Doo-da, doo-da.
I can eat all night. I can eat all day.
I can eat a twelve-hundred-pound bale of hay. Oooh, the doo-da-day."

Chassie looked at Milo and said, "You know Milo, Pony hasn't got all his marbles."

Milo looked at Chassie, "What do you mean?"

"I mean he's nuts!"

Milo wondered what "marbles" and "nuts" meant. *I better quit thinking; I am getting confused.*

The fairies said, "Milo, let's take a walk." They walked over to the fence.

Milo looked at the fence and said, "What's this about?"

"The fence protects Chassie, Breaker, and Pony. It keeps them in the pasture. You see, Milo, there are lots of dangers on the other side of this fence. Humans ride in things they call automobiles. They will run right over a horse and kill the horse and themselves. Humans are always in a hurry."

Milo said, "Why is that?"

"Humans really don't know. They are going nowhere fast!"

Milo said, "Oh, it's like Chassie says. They have lost their marbles. They are all nuts!"

The fairies said, "You got it, Milo! Well, let's get some sleep."

The fairies and Milo went to the edge of the woods and pulled the *Blanket of Sparkling Mist* over them. Then Milo thought about how beautiful the world was, and how the thought of humans disturbed him. *Almost seems like they really don't fit in!* Milo yawned and went to sleep.

The fairies woke Milo the next morning. It was just breaking daylight. The fairies spoke and said, "Milo, listen!" Milo heard the chain on the gate go clank! Milo looked across the field and at the gate. There was the human! Carrying a pail of water. The water that tasted like horse spit!

Milo said, "Holy Cow, they do walk on two legs! They are small!"

"Yes," the fairies said, "and remember, Milo, they are fragile."

Milo said, "Why do humans have horses?"

"Well, Milo, humans ride on horses' backs."

"Really?" Milo said.

"Yes, they do it for fun and enjoyment and, even now, they are used for some work. You see, Milo, horses were the main source of transportation years ago, before the car was invented."

Milo said, "Oh, that thing they run over horses with and go nowhere fast?"

"Yes, Milo," the fairies said. "The horse was also used for work. They pulled all the equipment for farming and for the growing of food. Now, we will tell you what else horses were used for—and it isn't good. They were used for war!"

Milo said, "What's war?"

"That's a game humans play. They kill each other for fame, fortune, and power."

Milo said, "Holy Cow, humans really don't fit in!"

"That's right Milo," the fairies said, "but there is hope for humans. There are a lot of humans who don't want war. If we could just get them to speak up! If we could just get everyone to live by the virtues: faith, hope, love, and charity. We could change the world, and then humans would fit in."

Milo had a very somber look on his face. He had never felt the weight of depression in his body before. *War! I have got to stop thinking about war! It is time to change the subject.*

The fairies said to Milo, "A new horse will come to the farm today."

"Holy Cow!" Milo said. "I will get to meet a new horse!"

"Yes, Milo, this day will be a day that you will never forget."

Milo and the fairies were in the balsam trees across the field. A truck with a horse trailer pulled into the farm. The humans unloaded the horse.

Milo couldn't believe what he saw! Milo said, "Fairies! Fairies! That horse looks like he's colored like me!" Milo began to shake.

The fairies said, "Milo, that horse is colored exactly like you! We painted him!"

Milo said, "I can't believe it!"

The fairies said, "Well, Milo, believe it! Everything about that horse is exactly like you, only his mind is different. He thinks differently than you and he cannot run as fast as the wind can blow."

Milo said, "What's his name?"

The fairies said, "His name is Mhilo."

Milo said, "He has even got the same name?"

The fairies said, "Well, it's spelled differently. If you want, you can pronounce it a little differently."

Milo was still shaking. He said, "I am really nervous. Can I just take a little walk?"

Milo walked through the balsam trees. He spoke to himself, "Holy Cow, I don't know what this is all about, but everything you do seems to turn out right in the end. So I accept it." A feeling of serenity came over Milo. He quit shaking and his nervousness went away.

He walked back to the fairies and said, "Fairies, I can't wait to meet Mhilo!" The fairies began to laugh, and Milo laughed with them.

Milo said, "This is the BEST of the BEST!"

The fairies said, "Milo, the family will be busy with the new horse today, so you will not get to meet him today."

The fairies and Milo walked through the woods. Milo said, "The trees are beautiful!"

Just then, Mr. Cool—the woodpecker—flew in and lit on a dead tree right next to Milo.

Milo said, "Hello, Mr. Cool."

Mr. Cool said, "Watch this, Milo." The dead bark and chips flew. It wasn't long before Mr. Cool had a hole three inches deep in the dead tree.

"How can you do that kind of pecking?" Milo asked. "That would give me a huge headache!"

Mr. Cool said, "Milo, we have a very special head. Our head has a strong, yet flexible bill. Our head has a hyoid structure of bone and elastic tissue that wraps around the skull (an area of spongy bone in the skull), and a little space for cerebral spinal fluid between the skull and the brain. I can strike a tree at 22 times a second with no injury to my brain."

Milo said, "You are a really sophisticated bird!"

Mr. Cool said, "Yes, you could say that! Us woodpeckers really have got a head on our shoulders!" And he chuckled.

Hyoid structure, spongy bone, cerebral spinal fluid between the skull and brain. Milo was getting confused. *I better quit thinking about a woodpecker's head.*

And he chuckled, "I bet humans wish they had heads like a woodpecker's. Then they would never have to wear head protection. Oh well, most humans don't wear it anyway. They would sooner die! Strange species I would say, and they only have two legs—poor things."

Mr. Cool pecked one more time and pulled a bug out of the hole. "I will take this bug and feed it to my children, Milo. I've got more pecking to do." And he flew away.

The fairies laughed. Milo laughed and said, "This is the BEST of the BEST!"

The fairies said, "Milo, let's get some sleep." So they pulled the *Blanket of Sparkling Mist* over him, and sat on Milo's nose, and went to sleep.

Milo had a dream. He dreamed about the horses that were used for cavalry. They were brave and strong and loyal. They were big and they were small.

He dreamed of the horses that were used for farming. They were big, heavy horses that could pull all day in the fields. Milo dreamed about the carriage hoses that were used for transportation of h umans. Milo laughed in his dream and said, "Those humans…they couldn't have made it without us horses."

## CHAPTER 5 | **TROUBLE WITH MHILO**

Milo awoke from his dream, looked down his nose, and saw the fairies were still there sleeping. Milo began to sing,

> "She'll be comin' round the mountain when she comes.
> She'll be comin' round the mountain when she comes.
> She'll be comin' round the mountain…"

The fairies awoke and began to sing with him. When they finished the song, they laughed and said, "What a great way to start a day! Well, I guess we should go see if the horses are awake yet."

They walked through the balsams and came to the edge of the field. Chassie, Breaker, and Pony were standing together. The new horse, Mhilo, was standing apart from them. The fairies said, "Mhilo, the new horse, is dominant."

Milo said, "What do you mean?"

"Mhilo will chase the other horses away from him if they get too close. He is not friendly."

Milo said, "I wonder why he's like that?"

The fairies said, "Some horses have a mean streak in their minds and they treat other horses badly."

Milo said, "Gee, he has got a real problem!"

The fairies said, "Yes, Milo, and it is our job to change him. Milo, when you walk up to him, be ready. He will touch noses with you and he will talk to you, but he will instantly try to dominate you."

Milo said, "I will be good to him but I will not tolerate meanness. I will not hurt him physically, and I will crush his meanness with love. I will humiliate him with action and not with words."

Milo and the fairies walked toward the horses. Milo felt a feeling of complete confidence. He knew that he would successfully achieve his goal to change Mhilo.

Milo reached the other horses. "Good morning, gang," he said.

Chassie said, "Well for sure it's morning, but I don't know if it's good!"

Milo said, "Chassie, I know what the problem is."

Chassie said, "Well, don't just stand there. Do something about it!"

Milo laughed and said, "Chassie, you are so-o-o-o-o bossy!"

Milo did a fast walk right toward Mhilo. Mhilo spun around to face him.

They came nose to nose. Milo spoke first, "Welcome to the farm."

Mhilo said, "Yeah, you look just like me!"

Milo said, "No-o-o. You look just like me!"

Mhilo said, "What are you? Some kind of wise guy?"

"No, I am a horse."

Mhilo looked right into Milo's eyes, and Milo looked right into Mhilo's eyes. They did not blink!

Mhilo said, "Tell you what, wise guy, I am going to give you the butt-kicking of a lifetime!"

Milo said, "I don't know why you keep calling me a 'wise guy.' I am a horse!"

Mhilo spun around and kicked at Milo. Milo side-stepped, and the kick missed.

Milo said, "Is that the best you can do?"

Mhilo came at Milo full speed, his teeth were bared. Milo jumped into the air and Mhilo ran right under him!

Milo said, "Mhilo, you should stop right now. You are making a fool of yourself."

Mhilo tried every aggressive move in the book of horse fighting, but he never touched Milo. Milo was too fast for him. (Remember, Milo could run as fast as the wind could blow!)

Milo said, "Mhilo, you are a terrific athlete. Why not use your skill for other things than fighting?"

Mhilo was out of breath. He paced back and forth. He felt the feeling of humiliation in his body.

Milo walked up to him and put his nose on Mhilo and said, "I love you. You are my brother."

Mhilo said, "No one has ever called me his brother," and tears rolled down his cheeks.

Milo said, "Us horses must always pull together, or we will never get the job of changing the world done."

Milo turned and walked over to Chassie, Breaker, and Pony, whose name was really Minute Man. They all had grins on their faces. Milo said, "You shouldn't grin because Mhilo was humiliated. I want you to be kind to him. Do not say anything to hurt him."

Pony said, "Ah gee, Milo! Can't I just taunt him a little bit?"

"What did I just tell you?"

"Ah gee, Milo, okay." Pony trotted away laughing.

Mhilo did not come over to the other horses. He walked across the field and, as he walked, the feeling of humiliation left his body. He walked to the top of the little hill. *No one has ever called me his brother or told me that they loved me.* He had never felt the feeling of love. It was the BEST of the BEST!

Mr. Cool came flying by. He circled around, came back, and lit on the electrical pole.

"Hi, Milo!" He said

Mhilo said, "I am not Milo. I am Mhilo."

Mr. Cool said, "You look just like Milo."

Mhilo said, "Yes, I do. We are brothers and we love each other."

Mr. Cool said, "All us male woodpeckers look alike, and we are brothers too. We love each other and we all fly together in hopes that we can change the world. Well, I got pecking to do." And he flew away.

Mhilo walked the fence line to see what the farm was like. It was a beautiful place. There were rabbits in the woods, also partridge and deer. He thought about how nice it would be to live in a place like this.

He walked over to the other horses. They were eating hay. They looked up. They all spoke up at the same time, "Welcome to our farm, Mhilo!"

Mhilo said, "Thanks," and took a bite of hay.

Chassie walked over to Mhilo. She said, "Those little girls you met yesterday will be riding you. I want you to be good to them."

"Oh, Chassie, I will be good to them and I will make them proud of me."

The fairies and Milo walked through the trees. It was a great day. Mhilo had learned about brotherhood and love. He would be a better horse for it.

Milo was tired.

The day's events were hard on Milo's nerves.

Milo lay down.

The fairies covered Milo with the *Blanket of Sparkling Mist.*

And Milo's eyes closed.

He began to dream. It was as if he was watching from above. The sun looked mystical and somewhat abstract. A horse that looked like Milo stood below. A beautiful black raven came flying in—he was mystical too and had a large wing-span. The bird lit on the horse's back. The horse jumped, and Milo jumped in his sleep.

The fairies laughed when Milo moved in his sleep. "He's dreaming. I wonder what about? Hope he remembers his dream. It will be quite interesting."

Milo's dream slipped away. When Milo awoke, the fairies asked him about his dream.

Milo said, "How did you know I was dreaming?"

"Milo, you were moving around in your sleep."

"Fairies, there was a horse in my dream. The horse looked like me. There was also a large, black bird. The bird lit on the horse's back."

The fairies looked at each other. They became silent, and then they totally changed the subject.

Milo looked at the fairies. "Why are you changing the subject? Let's discuss this further."

"Well…okay, Milo." The fairies began, "Milo, that dream you had about the horse and the bird…well, Milo, the horse was your father."

"My father?"

"Yes, Milo, and the bird was his companion. The Holy Cow created both of them. She gave them many supernatural gifts. The Top Being ordered her to send them to a different galaxy. The galaxy was controlled by evil.

"They were handed the Supreme Battle. They would have to defeat evil. The battle has been going on for a long time now; they are in the clean-up phase. When they are completely finished, they will return to the dimension you were born in."

"You mean I will meet my father some day?"

"Yes, Milo, and the bird too."

## CHAPTER 6 | **MILO MEETS RAVEN**

A raven circled overhead. Milo looked up, "Fairies, look at that bird!"

The fairies said, "Yes, Milo, that is a raven. That bird is super smart!"

Milo said, "He sure looks different from a woodpecker!"

The raven swooped down and lit on Milo's back. Milo jumped! It startled him.

The fairies laughed, "That raven likes you!"

Milo started to laugh.

The raven looked at Milo and said, "What's so funny?'

Milo said, "What's your name?"

In a sing-song voice, the raven replied,

"Raven is my name.

I am always looking for dead game.

I bet you think that's a shame!"

Milo said, "No, Raven, if it wasn't for you, the world would be a stinky place."

"You got it, Milo." Raven said. "Where are you headed?"

The fairies said, "We are going back to the dimension we came from. We need a vacation!"

Raven said, "Can I come along?"

The fairies said, "We are going back to Mirror Lake; but, Raven, you better bring some food with you because there's nothing for you to eat."

Raven said, "Okay, I will be right back!"

He flew away and grabbed a feed sack that was by the barn. He flew to the road and picked up all the dead game on the road that the humans ran over—going nowhere fast! He flew back to the fairies and Milo and said, "Let's move out!"

"Yes sir, Raven!" They began to march and sing,

> "Heigh-Ho! Heigh-Ho! Off to Mirror Lake we go.
> We are going to jump right in
> and take a swim.
> Heigh-Ho! Heigh-Ho! Heigh-Ho! Heigh-Ho!"

The fairies said, "Raven, fly ahead and look for a portal. You will smell clean, fresh air. That will be it."

Raven flew ahead and soon he was back. "I found the portal! It's about ten miles ahead."

The fairies and Raven jumped on Milo's back and away they went. Milo could jump the fences with ease. There were no obstacles that they could not conquer (Remember, the Arch Fairies, Mika and Joan, were super strong!). The group was unstoppable! They reached the portal in record time.

Raven said, "It is right here!"

The fairies covered it with the *Blanket of Sparkling Mist* and they rode Milo into his dimension.

Milo's dimension was so different than the world. There were rolling hills that were all different colors. The air was so fresh and clean it made you feel wide-awake. The smell of the air was unexplainable.

Raven said, "Holy Cow, this is unbelievable!" Raven took off from Milo's back. He flew higher and higher. Soon he was a black speck in the sky, and then he made a dive toward Milo and the fairies. They heard the thunder as he broke the sound barrier.

Milo said, "I hope he will be able to pull out of that dive!"

The fairies said, "Mika and Joan, get ready to save him if he can't."

Raven started to open his wings to slow down. He hollered out, "DON'T WORRY ABOUT ME; I

HAVE DONE THIS MANY TIMES!" Raven slowed and resumed normal flight. He came in and landed on Milo's back.

Milo said, "Raven, I thought you were done for!"

Raven laughed, "Milo, you ain't seen nothing yet!"

The fairies said, "We are about five miles from Mirror Lake. We will rest here."

They pulled the *Blanket of Sparkling Mist* over Milo. Raven sat on Milo's back, the fairies sat on his nose, and they all went to sleep.

Milo had a dream as he slept. It was about Raven. Raven had flown over 750 miles per hour that day, with no problems. He told Milo, "You ain't seen nothing yet."

This raven must not be from the world. When Milo looked at him he got a feeling that maybe he was from another dimension. Could he have come from the Special Place? Could the Holy Cow have sent him to us?

Milo prayed in his sleep, "Holy Cow, if you sent Raven to us, I want to thank you." And Milo's dream went away.

It was morning. Raven unfolded his wings, stretched, and said, "Man, I slept good! Milo makes a much better bed that sleeping in an old tree. Hey…I haven't seen any trees!"

The fairies woke up, "Good morning, Raven."

Milo was still sleeping. The fairies began to sing that beautiful song, the song from the Special Place. Raven joined in. *How does he know this song?* The fairies wondered.

They stopped singing, but Raven kept on. They waited until he finished. "Raven, how do you know this song? No one from the world knows this song!"

Raven said, "Well…Ahhh…Like I said, you ain't seen nothing yet!" And he laughed.

This laugh was nothing like the fairies had ever heard. It was full of strange sounds.

The fairies said, "That's how ravens laugh?"

Raven said, "Yeah! Sounds better than the way you fairies laugh!" and he hopped straight up in the air.

This woke up Milo. He stood up and stretched, "Good morning, everyone, let's go to Mirror Lake."

Raven said, "It is time for breakfast," and he opened his feed sack.

Milo and the fairies gagged from the smell!

Raven said, "It smells good to me!" He ate breakfast.

When Raven had finished, he said, "Let's go to Mirror Lake." Then he let out a big burp! He blew his breath on Milo and the fairies, and they gagged again!

Raven laughed, but continued, "You ain't seen nothing yet!" Raven flew in front of Milo and the fairies. He let out a huge fart!

The stink was so bad; Milo's eyes burned, his lips curled up, and he gagged again. The fairies fell of Milo's back and they muttered, "We have been gassed!!!!"

Raven laughed until tears rolled down his cheeks. *They don't know I'm the farting champion of the Fourth Dimension!*

While Raven was laughing, Mika and Joan grabbed the feed sack, flew away, and buried it. When they got back, Raven said, "Why did you do that?"

Mika and Joan said, "Raven, you have no manners and, now, we are going to teach you some."

Raven became defiant.

Mika and Joan said, "Listen, Raven, you have no choice. You are going to learn manners, or we are going to pluck you bald!"

Milo said, "Raven, you better listen to Mika and Joan. They have never backed down on their word. They are very strong fairies and can handle everything except Mother Nature."

Raven hung his head, "I am sorry that I have no manners. Mika and Joan, will you teach me?" Mika and Joan laughed. Their laugh was beautiful. It was in harmony (remember, they both speak at the same time). "We will teach you."

Milo thought about how intelligent Raven was. If he or humans knew everything Raven knew, it would be a blessing. Raven was a beautiful bird! His blackness did not impress humans, but it sure impressed Milo. His flying ability was second to none. His speech was so different, and the sounds he made were unbelievable, and now he knew Raven had come to them from the Holy Cow.

Mika and Joan finished teaching Raven manners, they never prolong things. They always get right to business. "We are finished," they said, "let's go to Mirror Lake."

Raven flew ahead. He was the head scout. In the distance he saw a blinding glitter. It was Mirror Lake. He flew back to Milo and said, "There are two miles to go."

Milo broke into a trot, and it wasn't long before they were at Mirror Lake. The water was beautiful.

The fairies said, "Raven, if you drink from Mirror Lake, you will never have to eat again; for the water from Mirror Lake is the gift of life!"

Raven dipped his beak into the water, put his head back, and swallowed. He couldn't believe how good it was! He had never tasted water like it! He thought, *This is truly the gift of life!*

The Arch Fairies jumped into the water. They swam and played. They said, "Hey, Milo, come on in!"

Milo said, "Wait a minute!" But the Arch Fairies jumped out of the water, grabbed Milo, picked him up, and threw him in. Milo began to swim (If Milo could run as fast as the wind can blow, how fast could he swim? Could he swim as fast as a dolphin? We will never know unless his travels bring him to an ocean). Everyone enjoyed the lake. They spent the day there.

Milo, Raven, and the fairies said, "We will spend the night here." They covered themselves with the *Blanket of Sparkling Mist* and went to sleep.

Raven dreamed about trees. He missed them very much. He thought, *There have got to be trees in this dimension! If I can just find them…* And his dream went away.

CHAPTER 7 | **THE UNBELIEVABLE FOREST**

Milo awoke. There the fairies were, sitting on his nose. They were truly beautiful and, oh! How small they were! Mika and Joan slept on top of each nostril, but they slept standing. Milo realized that he hadn't spent much time observing the fairies. They were such unique life-forms. They could look like humans if they wanted, and when they did, they looked this way:

Mika and Joan were very muscular in build.

Charity was quite plain looking. But the more he looked at her, he noticed she was a perfect specimen—who looked like she had been carved from a piece of granite.

Love was almost angelic looking. Her looks and size seemed to change every ten seconds.

Faith was tall—for a fairy anyway—and very thin. She looked fragile.

Hope was short, shorter than all the other fairies, with a face that was beautiful.

They were all so beautiful in their own way and they all had only two legs. *Poor things!* Milo woke up the fairies and said, "Watch this!" Milo rolled on his back with his feet stuck up in the air.

The fairies jumped from one hoof to the other. This was the BEST of the BEST!

Joan and Mika said, "Hey! Where's Raven? Has anyone seen him?"

Everyone said, "No" at the same time. But then they spotted a black speck coming toward them. It was Raven coming in on a low-level flight. He pulled up and set down.

Milo said, "Where have you been, Raven?"

"I was out looking for trees. Didn't find any!"

Just then, Wind came over the hill. Milo shouted out, "Hey Wind, do you know if there are any trees in this dimension?"

"Trees?" Wind asked. "Boy do I ever!"

Raven perked up, "Where are they?"

"The trees are 500 miles due north."

"Thanks," Raven said, "man, do I ever need to sit in a tree!"

Milo said, "Hey fairies let's head for the trees."

Wind said, "Wait a minute! I want to show you something." Wind blew across Mirror Lake. The water shimmered and sparkled like a sea of diamonds. It was unbelievably beautiful!

The fairies, Milo, and Raven had never seen anything like it. Wind turned around and headed back toward Milo. It picked up speed. Soon, a wave four feet high came at Milo and the fairies. The water came clear up to Milo's belly.

Raven flew just high enough to be above the water. He used his wing and started splashing Milo.

Milo laughed.

Wind said, "See you later gang!" and blew away.

Milo said, "Let's head for the trees. If we average fifty miles an hour, in ten hours we will be there." Milo galloped at 50 miles per hour (His internal speedometer told him he was averaging 50.) Nine and one-half hours later, Mika and Joan spoke, "We see the tops of the trees!"

Milo stopped and said, "If that doesn't get me in shape, nothing will."

Raven said, "Let's rest!"

Everyone was exhausted. The fairies said, "Let's sleep here."

They pulled the *Blanket of Sparkling Mist* over themselves and went to sleep.

No one dreamed that night, they were all too tired!

Milo awoke the next morning. "Let's get up!" he hollered. Milo stood up; his muscles were stiff from that 475-mile run! He walked around, "I have got to loosen up!"

The fairies jumped on Milo's back. Milo took off on a fast walk. It would not be long before they would

reach the trees. They couldn't believe how tall the trees were! The trees were huge! Milo said, "I bet these trees are 1,000 feet tall!" The color of them was unbelievable! The tree trunks were spirals, and they were multi-colored.

Milo said to the fairies, "Have you ever seen a forest so beautiful, trees so big?"

The fairies looked for Raven. He lay on the ground behind Milo. He was so excited, he had fainted. "Wake up Raven! Wake up!" Mika and Joan grabbed him and shook him.

Raven awoke. Raven said, "This is unreal!" and he took off. He flew higher and higher until he reached the tops of the trees. The tops were iridescent in color. They seemed to sparkle and change color as he looked across the tops. He circled and came down to Milo and the fairies. He could not speak! He started to cry! The trees were so beautiful! It took a few minutes for Raven to regain his composure. Raven's first words were, "This is the BEST of the BEST!"

Milo and the fairies danced around. They grabbed Raven and gave him a big hug. Joan and Mika threw him up in the air, and Raven flew around them.

All of a sudden, they heard a thumping sound! They all stopped. Milo said, "What was that?'

Mika and Joan came to attention. They stopped dead in their tracks. Thump! Thump! The surface shook. Thump! Thump!

Milo said, "Whatever it is, it's big!"

The hair on Milo's back stood on end. Milo started to shake. Mika and Joan seemed quite unconcerned. (Remember, there is nothing they can't handle. Only Mother Nature can get the best of them.)

Thump!

Thump!

The sound got closer…and closer….

Milo said, "Get ready. Here it comes!"

And from out of the forest came a large snowshoe rabbit. When her feet hit the ground, it sounded like thunder. The rabbit spoke, "Hi folks! Scared the living daylights out of you, didn't I?" And she laughed until she cried.

Milo took a deep breath, "What're you doing here?"

"I'm the keeper of the forest."

Milo said, "You?"

And Rabbit said, "Yeah, just because I'm a rabbit doesn't mean I can't take care of the trees." And she jumped up and boxed Milo's ears.

Milo said, "Man, my ears are touchy!"

Rabbit said, "I know. All horses have touchy ears."

Milo said, "What do you know about horses?"

Rabbit said, "I know more about horses than you do!"

Milo said, "How is that?"

Rabbit said, "Have you ever heard about a horse called Chassie?"

Milo said, "You mean the horse who lives in the world?"

"Yes," Rabbit said, "I have been communicating with her for thirty-three years. You see, Milo, Chassie has extrasensory perception and she is telepathic, clairvoyant, and all that other good stuff. I have never seen her, but she always talks to me."

Milo said, "Yes, Rabbit, she is quite an old horse."

Rabbit said, "She is one of a kind."

Milo said, "What keeps these trees alive?"

"Well," Rabbit said, "the roots go 2,000 feet deep into an aquifer. It's the same water that feeds Mirror Lake. And the best part of it is, this dimension has no humans in it. You know the humans would drill into it and wreck it."

While Rabbit and Milo were talking, Raven was flying through the trees. He loved it. Raven thought, *I*

*haven't seen any forms of life, no other birds…nothing!* He flew back to Milo and Rabbit. He said, "You are very large!"

Rabbit said, "But look at my feet!" She pulled her feet from under her furry body. They were as long as her whole body! She said, "How do you like these snowshoes?"

Raven said, "Does it snow here?"

Rabbit said, "Only in the trees. They are so tall they make their own weather."

Raven said, "Do you live here alone?"

"Yes," Rabbit said.

"Don't you get lonesome?" Raven asked.

"Sometimes I do, and that's when I talk to Chassie, but otherwise I am busy taking care of the trees."

The fairies said, "Rabbit, are there any mountains?"

Rabbit shook her head, "Yes! The mountains are thousands of feet high and it is very cold there. So cold, you could never survive."

Milo and the fairies were very tired.

Raven said, "I will sleep in the trees." He flew off.

Milo said, "Rabbit, do you want to sleep under the *Blanket of Sparkling Mist?*"

Rabbit said, "Oh no. I will sleep in my den."

Milo and the fairies pulled the *Blanket of Sparkling Mist* over them and went to sleep.

Milo and the fairies awoke to the sound of a symphony orchestra. It wasn't very loud. It was easy on the ears. But anyhow the fairies said, "Milo, it's coming from the trees."

There was a slight breeze blowing through the trees. Wind had come during the night and he was playing the trees. It was beautiful!

The snowshoe rabbit came out of the trees. Her footsteps were now silent.

Milo said, "Rabbit, you can walk so loudly and also so quietly!"

"Yes, Milo, when the trees are sleeping, I do not want to awaken them. They get stressed out! I baby these trees. They love to be coddled."

Raven came out of the trees. He flew in rhythm to the music. It was a sight to behold. He flew back and forth over Milo's head.

*What a talent Raven has!*

The music stopped. Wind came out of the trees and gave a bow. The fairies, Milo, and Rabbit gave him a standing ovation. Wind bowed again and blew away.

Milo said, "Raven, that was beautiful the way you flew to the music!"

"Thanks Milo, but you ain't seen nothing yet!"

Then Raven said, "I once went to an air show when I was in the world. The humans have flying machines. They call them airplanes. The airplanes were big and they were small, and they all made so much noise that your ears would hurt."

Milo said, "Man, I hate my ears to hurt!"

Raven continued, "They flew around, and the people went ooohhh and aaahhh. I watched from a distance. I was not impressed. Humans never ooohhh and aaahhh when us ravens fly around…and we don't hurt anyone's ears!

"And then they brought out the aerobatic airplanes. They had short wings and big engines, and boy, were they noisy! They did their maneuvers, and I copied every move they made. I did it with hardly any noise, only the whoosh of my wings."

When the airplanes finished and landed, Raven kept flying. He did tricks that would rip the wings right off the airplanes, but humans did not notice. Most humans are wrapped up in worldly things. They never really do look at nature.

Raven said, "Milo, fairies, Rabbit, remember when I dove and broke the sound barrier? And then I said, 'you ain't seen nothing yet?' Well, watch this!"

Raven jumped straight up and started flying. He did every trick in the aerobatic flight book and much more. Straight up, backwards, sideways, flips, loops, cartwheels, and then he hovered. But then, he started to climb. Soon he was a black speck. Soon, he was out of sight.

And then everyone heard the sonic boom! It echoed through the trees like a huge bass drum. Raven had broken the sound barrier! They looked up. A black speck appeared.

"Mach one! Mach two! Mach three!" Milo shouted. "He will never be able to pull out at that speed!"

Raven did not open his wings. He bent his tail and began to make his turn. When he went over Milo, the fairies, and Rabbit, the wind from the speed tumbled them across the surface! The gang was speechless! Raven flew back and lit on a branch. "Well, did I impress you?" And he laughed.

Milo could not speak, but he thought how Raven was truly from a Special Place, and how he had been anointed by the Holy Cow. *Thank you, Holy Cow, for letting us meet him.*

The fairies said, "Milo, it is time to move on."

Milo said, "Yes, I suppose so." He really didn't want to leave. The trees had a magnetic effect on him.

Rabbit said, "You really don't want to leave, do you Milo? It's the trees Milo. They have great powers. They like to test your willpower. If you stayed here, your life would be easy and trouble free, and no one would fault you for it. If you leave here, your life will be full of challenges, like the Mhilo challenge that you executed flawlessly."

Milo raised his head high and said, "I will leave." The fairies jumped on Milo.

Raven said, "I will stay. There are some things that the trees can teach me. I will catch up with you later."

Milo said, "Okay. See you later." And Milo trotted off.

## CHAPTER 8 | **BRAVO AND MANDIE**

Milo and the fairies set their course for southwest. They came over a hill and looked out over a flat plain. The plain was in the shape of a huge guitar. The flat plain had a laminated look down the center. The lines were tan and brown. Milo followed the lines. They were pointed southwest.

The fairies said, "These lines remind us of strings on a guitar."

The surface was flat. It felt good on Milo's hooves.

Wind came over the hill and began to pick at the strings. Wind did a little tuning, and said, "This is a song for you. It is called 'Ghost Riders in the Sky.'"

The music had a strange effect on Milo. He broke into a gallop.

Milo and the Arch Fairies began to sing. Their voices were perfect for the song. Wind played every note. Milo and the Arch Fairies sang every word.

When they finished the song, Milo stood on his hind legs and let out a huge whinny in a tribute to the horses in the song. The whinny echoed across the plain.

The fairies hollered out, "Bravo!" Joan and Mika took a bow.

Milo said, "This is the BEST of the BEST!"

*The fairies hollered out, "BRAVO." Why does that word stick in my mind?*

Milo and the fairies continued on the journey. It was only a short walk, and then they would be back into hilly country.

The fairies said, "Look at the size of those hills!" They were huge! Milo started up the hill and the fairies held on. Up and down they went. It was good that Milo had such strong legs. The hills didn't seem to be a challenge for him. They reached a flat field of green grass.

Milo thought this must have been the field he dreamed about running in. In the middle of the field was a spring. He smelled the water. It smelled like the water in Mirror Lake. He took a drink. It tasted like the water in Mirror Lake. Milo said, "Fairies, this water is safe."

The fairies all took a drink. It was the BEST of the BEST!

The fairies said, "We will stop here." They pulled the *Blanket of Sparkling Mist* over Milo, sat on his nose, and went to sleep.

Milo did not dream that night. Morning came and the fairies did not touch Milo's ears. They scratched Milo under his chin.

Milo awoke. "Boy does that feel good!" Milo jumped up. "Let's move out!" And away they went.

All of a sudden, Faith said, "Stop. I smell horse poop!"

Milo said, "There must be a portal here."

The fairies sniffed around, "It's right here!" They put the *Blanket of Sparkling Mist* over it, and Milo stuck his head through the hole.

The fairies said, "It's the world again!"

There was a big, long-legged horse and a small horse, a little bigger than a pony. Milo pulled his head out of the hole and said, "Let's stop and talk to them."

The fairies said, "Open the hole bigger, we will ride in." And they did.

The horses lived inside a small, fenced-in area. They looked up to see Milo. They came walking over. They smelled Milo.

Milo said, "Milo is my name."

"My name is Bravo," the big horse said, "and this is Mandie."

Mandie said, "Hi, handsome!"

"No, my name is Milo."

Mandie reached out and gave Milo a lick.

The fairies giggled.

Milo ignored Mandie. He said, "Bravo. That's a cool name!"

Bravo said, "Thanks. My great-grandfather was a famous racehorse. His name was Dash for Cash. There's a statue of him in the Quarter Horse Hall of Fame in Texas."

Milo said, "Really? Are you a race horse?"

Bravo said, "I was one when I was younger."

Milo said, "Did you win any races?"

"No, Milo, I came in second once. I could've won, but I held back. I didn't want to hurt the other horse's feelings."

Milo said, "Good for you, Bravo! You are a very kind horse."

Bravo said, "You know, Milo, those humans used us horses to make money by betting."

Milo said, "What's money?"

Bravo said, "Money is the ROOT of all evil! Humans say this, yet they strive for it. Humans are weird beings."

Milo said, "Tell me about it!"

"They also drive automobiles, but they are going nowhere fast!"

Milo and Bravo shook their heads and chuckled. While Bravo and Milo were talking, Mandie was giving Milo that evil woman's eye.

Milo said, "Mandie, you can quit now."

Mandie said, "Okay Milo, Honey," and she gave him another lick.

*That word "honey"... wonder why the word "honey" rings a bell in my mind?*

Bravo said, "Alright, Mandie, that's enough!"

Mandie walked away swishing her tail.

Milo said, "She sure is strange!" And the fairies giggled.

Bravo said, "Milo, have you ever been in a parade?"

Milo said, "What's a parade?"

Bravo said, "A parade is an event that humans ride us horses in to show us off. People line both sides of the road, and we walk down the road. They stand there and look at us, and does it ever make me nervous!"

Milo said, "I was nervous once and I just shook! It was the first time I had seen Mhilo. Mhilo looked just like me!"

Bravo said, "That would make me nervous, too."

Milo said, "But I just talked to the Holy Cow, and she just calmed me right down."

Bravo said, "I have heard of the Holy Cow, but I have never tried to talk to her."

Milo said, "Just say, 'Holy Cow, please help me,' and she will calm you right down. Bravo, have you ever seen yourself?"

Bravo said, "No."

Milo said, "I have seen myself in Mirror Lake. You know, Bravo, we are a magnificent species! Our heads are beautiful; our legs are long and strong. We are of many colors. We are superior to humans. Our minds are pure and clean.

"Humans take us for granted. They think we are dumb because we do not speak their language. We are loyal to other horses AND to humans. Humans are not a loyal species. That is why they are constantly at war. That's why they do not like each other. They always put themselves first."

Mandie said, "Hey Milo, what happened to you? It looks like someone threw bleach on you!"

Bravo said, "Mandie, Milo is a Paint, because he is two colors. The white extends over his back."

Mandie said, "It looks quite neat!"

Milo said, "Thanks, Mandie! You are a small horse."

Mandie said, "Yes, Milo, I am part Quarter Horse and part pony."

Milo said, "I know a pony. His name is Minute Man, but usually I call him Pony! It's what humans say is a nickname. Kind of confusing, so I don't think about it much."

Mandie said, "Milo, have you ever worn a harness?"

Milo said, "No, what's that?"

Mandie said, "It's a leather thing that humans put on horses, so humans can hook things on it, and pull them around. It's what the big workhorses wear. It is fun to pull things, Milo. There is something about pulling things that we horses like. You should try it sometime."

Milo said, "Maybe I will, it sounds like fun!"

Bravo said, "Mandie, you talk too much."

Mandie said, "Well Bravo, you were a nervous wreck until I came here to keep you company." Bravo said, "Yeah, I know! Milo, I wish I could go with you, but Theresa would miss me so much. She would cry and I would miss her. Theresa is a human, a woman, sometimes called a *lady*."

Milo said, "Does she have only two legs?"

Bravo answered, "Yes, Milo, all humans have only two legs. Poor things!"

Milo said, "Yes, I really feel sorry for humans. They are so fragile. But now, Bravo, I must move on." And Milo began to sing, "So long. It's been good to know you…" and Bravo joined in.

The fairies waved goodbye to Mandie.

Mandie hollered out, "Goodbye, Milo Honey!"

Milo said, "Gee, is she sickening!"

The fairies giggled. They said in their quiet little voices, "Move out, Milo honey!"

Milo bucked, and Faith, Hope, Love, and Charity fell off and landed in a big mud puddle. Mika and Joan were too agile. They held on to Milo's ears.

Milo said, "Sorry about that, ladies!" (It was the first time Milo had called the fairies 'ladies'. The Mandie thing had really confused him!) "You are not going to get on me looking like that! You have to get cleaned up!"

The fairies were going to scold Milo, but the look in his eyes was a look of firmness AND a look of kindness. They had never seen that look before. The fairies felt his presence. His stature was magnificent! Milo had a heart of gold and a soul of fire! Milo had become a horse they could trust with their lives! Milo would be their Guardian.

## CHAPTER 9 | **THE HONEY BEE AND INFERNO**

Milo said, "Well, fairies, let's try it again,"

The magically sparkling clean fairies jumped on Milo's back. They hollered out, "Let's move out!" And Milo took off at a gallop. They would be looking for a portal to get back into their dimension. Milo opened his nostrils wide to see if he could smell the clean, fresh air.

The Arch Fairies flew ahead of Milo. All of a sudden, the Arch Fairies stopped. Milo almost ran over them. *That was a close call! I must be more careful!*

The Arch Fairies said, "This is it!" They put the *Blanket of Sparkling Mist* over the hole. Milo stuck his head through the hole and couldn't believe what he saw. Milo was looking at a huge blanket of flowers. It stretched as far as he could see! Rolling hills of flowers! Different colors. Different patterns. He was awestruck!

The fairies said, "Milo, we have never seen such beauty! Milo, pull your head out of the hole."

Milo pulled his head out of the hole. The fairies stretched the *Blanket of Sparkling Mist* over the hole and rode Milo into their dimension.

Milo looked around in awe and said, "This is the BEST of the BEST."

He walked through the flowers. Milo and the fairies started laughing. The scent from the flowers made them laugh. They had a hard time stopping, but they finally got themselves under control.

Milo said, "Stop! Listen!" Milo's hearing was super keen. He could hear a buzzing sound. It got more intense by the second, and then a flying object came over the hill. It was yellow and black. It was the size of a baseball.

It was a beautiful honeybee! It lit on Milo's nose. "Hi, Milo!"

Milo said, "How do you know my name?"

"Milo, I know everything about you. I bet you can't guess who told me!"

Milo said, "Has a horse from the world been talking to you?"

The honeybee said, "Yes, the horse named Chassie."

Milo said, "Yes, I know Chassie. She talks to everyone!"

The honeybee said, "Milo, follow me."

Milo and the fairies followed the honeybee through the flowers. The scent of the flowers smelled so good and, every so often, they would start laughing. They walked for one mile and then they saw a huge "top" that was spinning slowly.

The honeybee hollered out, "That's my home!"

Milo said, "Whoa! That's BEAUTIFUL!" The "top" was multi-colored. It made him dizzy when he looked at it too long.

The honeybee said, "It's full of honey right now."

Milo said, "Who eats all that honey?"

The honeybee said, "I eat some of it, but most of it goes to the Special Place. The Holy Cow loves honey. She shares it with everyone who lives in the Special Place."

The fairies said, "Where are the other bees?"

"There ARE no other bees. I take care of the whole flower patch."

Milo said, "You have got to be kidding!"

"No," the bee said, "I never kid around. The Holy Cow made me that way. Milo, stick out your tongue." The bee laughed at the size of Milo's tongue. She put some honey on his tongue.

Milo tasted it and said, "That is the BEST of the BEST!"

Milo and the fairies all had a meal of honey. They thanked the bee. The fairies said, "Well, we'd better move out!" They jumped on Milo's back and waved goodbye.

They walked until they got to the edge of the flower patch. The fairies said, "We will camp here."
They pulled the *Blanket of Sparkling Mist* over Milo and went to sleep.

Milo and the fairies slept late. The honey had made them extra sleepy. They stretched and started laughing. The honey in their bellies made them full of joy.

Milo said, "Well, we'd better get on the move!"

As they headed southwest, the terrain became quite flat. The colors changed to gray, black, and purple. The sky had lightning bolts in it, but there was no sound. It was dead quiet!

The fairies said, "This is sure different!"

When Milo's feet hit the ground, they gave off a ringing sound. It was as if he was walking on steel. Everyone was quiet as they walked along. Milo had a strange feeling enter his body. His muscles tightened.

The fairies became nervous, but not Mika and Joan. They were little pillars of strength. They even had smiles on their faces. Something was going to happen and they loved it!

Milo stopped. "Be quiet, fairies." His ears turned back and forth, and then they stopped. They were homed in on one direction. He could hear the sound of a horse walking. It was a long ways away. Milo sniffed the air. It had a faint burning smell to it. It smelled like hot steel.

Milo said, "Fairies, I want you to be really quiet." And Milo started walking toward the sound. Milo walked for one mile at a steady pace. The smell of hot steel became more intense. Milo stopped. His eyes scanned the landscape. He could not see anything—just gray, black, and purple. The lightning bolts raced across the sky. The air was dead still.

Milo said, "I KNOW there is something watching me. I just can't make it out."

Milo walked ahead. *I wonder if I can get it to show itself?*

Milo broke into a gallop. He was running at fifty miles per hour, and then he came to a sliding stop as his hooves screeched against the ground. Or was it steel? It just had a thin layer of powder on it.

Milo listened, and then he heard a horse coming at full gallop. It was coming straight at him, and then it appeared! The horse was one-half mile away! He was colored gray, black, and purple. His color blended into the surroundings. The horse was coming straight at Milo.

*He is closing the distance.* It looked to Milo like he was going as fast as forty miles per hour.
The horse was big, tall, and heavy. Milo thought that the horse must weigh 4,000 pounds! The horse was now at one-quarter mile. Milo could see his eyes. They changed color. First, they looked like diamonds and then they looked like rubies. The horse's color then began to brighten. The horse began to glow, his color no longer matching the surroundings.

The fairies hollered out, "Holy Cow, please spare us!" Mika and Joan sang, "Mine eyes have seen the glory of the coming of the Cow," and they broke out laughing.

The big horse was fifty yards from Milo. When the big horse was eight feet from Milo, Milo sidestepped, and the big horse went by him like a locomotive! The fairies screamed! Milo got a big grin on his face. The big horse came to a screeching halt, spun around, reared up, and came at Milo again! Milo stood his ground. The big horse was breathing fire! Smoke came out of his nostrils! Milo jumped into the air, and the big horse ran right under him. The battle went on for fifteen minutes and, finally, the big horse stopped.

He looked at Milo and said, "Where in the heck did you learn to move like *THAT*?"

Milo said, "The Holy Cow made me this way. I can run as fast as the wind can blow."

The big horse's voice was like Thunder!

Milo said, "Boy, does that hurt my ears!"

"Sorry 'bout that. I will try to speak a little softer. I am used to speaking loud. When we were in battle, it was noisy. I had to speak like that so the other horses could hear me."

The big horse started laughing. Milo started laughing. The fairies started laughing.

Mika and Joan flew off Milo's back, flew under the big horse, and picked him up off the ground.

The big horse said, "You are Arch Fairies. Only Arch Fairies could do this," and he let out a huge whinny.

Milo said, "What's your name?"

"My name is Inferno," and the big horse pawed the ground.

"My name is Milo. It's great to meet you, Inferno! I have a question for you. If I wouldn't have side-stepped, would you have run over me?"

"Yes, Milo, I would have plowed you right over. The Holy Cow made ME that way! I am a cavalry horse. I fought in all the great cavalry wars."

Milo said, "I do not know anything about those wars."

Inferno said, "I will teach you everything about those wars, I was a heavy cavalry horse. The Holy Cow sent me into the wars to teach me what the world was like. She gave me the gift of eternal life."

Milo said, "She gave me that gift, too! She also wants me to spread faith, hope, love, and charity into the world."

Inferno said, "That's why I have met you, Milo. I will teach you what the world is like when it comes to war." Inferno told Milo about all the great horses of war and how they suffered and died for humans.

Milo cried as he heard the stories.

Inferno said, "Oh, Milo, those horses all went to see the Holy Cow and now they will live in peace with her."

Inferno schooled Milo in all the philosophical teachings of a just war. When he did this, he put his forehead against Milo's forehead and transferred these teachings in Milo's mind. St. Augustine. Thomas Aquinas. The School of Salamanca. Just war doctrine of the Catholic Church. Indian Epic Mahabharata.

Milo was amazed at what Inferno had done. When Inferno finished, he looked right into Milo's eyes, and spoke these words. "Milo Boy, you ain't seen nothing yet."

Inferno also taught Milo about all the wars that had taken place in the world. He told about the use of atom bombs and everything, right up to the use of drones. Milo was overwhelmed with grief.

Inferno said, "Milo, you have to get used to the wicked things in the world. Go forth and spread the word of faith, hope, love, and charity."

## CHAPTER 10 | **AZURA AND BURNT FEATHERS**

At that moment, Milo heard a sound behind him. He spun around in a flash! There was something coming toward him. It was a bluish, white glow. It hurt his eyes when he looked at it. By the sound, it was another horse. Milo positioned himself for another battle.

Inferno said, "Relax, Milo, it's my mate."

A beautiful, bluish-white Arabian mare came forth. She looked like a piece of fine bone china. Her eyes were the color of amethyst. She was a sight to behold!

"Her name is Azura!"

Milo gave a bow and said, "It is a pleasure to meet you, Azura."

Inferno said, "Milo's mission is to go into the world and teach love, faith, hope and charity."

Azura said, "Milo, I have never seen a horse colored like you!"

Milo said, "I am a Buckskin Paint. There is a horse that looks just like me who lives in the world, and his name is Mhilo."

Azura swished her tail up and down, and two small horses appeared in the distance. They came running in and stood by their mother. One was a filly and one was a colt. The filly was black and the colt was white.

Inferno stepped forward looking at the little tykes. "Little tykes they are, eh, Milo?"

Milo spoke, "Yes, Inferno, little tykes they are!"

The fairies flew to the filly and the colt. They tickled their noses and it made them laugh. The two young horses jumped over each other's backs as they ran. Milo and Inferno laughed.

Azura hollered out, "Be careful now!"

Inferno, Milo, and Azura talked about what a bleak place they were in. The black, gray, and purple place was very depressing.

Milo asked, "Do you always live here?"

Azura said, "Oh no, Milo. We travel all over this dimension; this dimension is a wonderful place!"

Milo asked, "Have you ever seen the mountains?"

Inferno said, "Only from a distance. We were about 300 miles from them, and it was very cold, so we turned back and headed south to warmer weather."

Azura said, "I have heard that it gets 250 fifty degrees below zero there."

The fairies said, "Milo, we must leave." They jumped on Milo's back and said their goodbyes, and Milo trotted off.

They traveled for four hours. The landscape did not change. The lightning bolts raced across the sky. *I hope things change pretty quickly! I am really sick of this place,* thought Milo. Finally, the purple went away, then the black, and then the gray. The lightning bolts subsided. There was a light green haze ahead. Milo trotted on into the haze.

The smell was of freshly mown grass. It was wonderful! Even though Milo did not have to eat, his mouth watered. They trotted out of the haze and into a beautiful field of green grass. The grass was twelve inches high!

Wind was there. "Hi, Milo! Welcome to this wonderful place! Taste this grass."

Milo reached down and smelled the grass. It was the best smell! He took a bite and it tasted wonderful! Milo said, "Oh, Wind, this is wonderful!"

Wind said, "Do not eat too much of this grass, it could make you sick. Horses founder on grass like this." Milo thought the words "sick" and "founder" sounded serious. *I will take Wind's advice. He seems very intelligent.*

"Hey Wind, have you seen Raven?"

"Yes, I have. He is looking for you."

"If you see him, tell him where we are."

"I will!" And Wind blew away.

Milo lay down in the grass. It felt good. He rolled onto his back. "Boy, this is great!" Milo rolled over and over. He was so agile he could do it easily. He jumped up and shook himself.

The fairies landed on Milo's back and said, "Milo, you smell like fresh grass!"

Milo laughed and then began to sing one of his horse songs. Milo's horse song echoed across the field of green. (Oh, yes, that Milo, he really aims to please!) Milo's voice was beautiful.

The fairies joined in. It was wonderful! And some day they would sing for the Holy Cow. They finished their song and began to laugh. They were so happy!  Milo became silent. He raised his head high. His ears rotated back and forth. He picked up on a strange sound. Milo said, "Fairies, listen! I think I hear Raven."

It WAS Raven. The sound he was making was stressful. They could not see him yet. He was too far away. Milo stood still. He sniffed the air. He could smell burned feathers. "I can't see Raven, but I think he is in trouble."

Raven's call was getting closer. Then Milo spotted him. He was flying just above the grass. He looked hurt. Milo went running towards him. Raven landed. Mika and Joan picked him up and set him on Milo's back. His feathers were all singed. He looked terrible.

Milo said, "What happened to you?"

Raven spoke, "I flew through the black, gray, and purple place. I got hit by lightning. I didn't think I was going to make it…"and he fainted.

The fairies said, "We must clean him up and administer first-aid. Milo, eat some of that green grass and hold back saliva. We will need it to clean up Raven."

The fairies flew back and forth from Milo's mouth to Raven and washed him with the green saliva. When they were done, they wrapped Raven in Milo's mane, and Raven slept.

The fairies said, "We will sleep here." They pulled the *Blanket of Sparkling Mist* over Milo, sat by Raven, and went to sleep.

Raven dreamed he had lost all his feathers. He could not fly. He could only hop around. He was helpless! He started to cry in his sleep.

The fairies awoke. They had heard his crying. They gathered around Raven and began to hum a very different song.

Then Raven awoke. He listened to the song. It made him feel much better. He said, "Fairies, do you think I will ever get my feathers back?"

The fairies said, "Raven, look at yourself. Your feathers are all new."

Raven spread his wings. His shiny, new feathers looked beautiful. "WOW! I can't believe it!"

"Well, believe it, Raven! You look great!" and the fairies laughed.

Raven hollered out, "Milo! Milo! Wake up! Look at me!"

Milo jumped up and Raven flew around his head. His new feathers sparkled!

Milo said, "Amazing what a little horse spit will do!" and he laughed.

The fairies said, "Well, it's time to move out!" They and Raven climbed on Milo's back, and he trotted off.

Milo was trotting at a brisk pace when he heard his name. "M-i-l-o! M-i-l-o!"

He came to an abrupt halt. The fairies almost fell off his back. Milo said, "Did you hear that?"

The fairies said "No. What did you hear?"

"Someone called out my name!"

"M-i-l-o! M-i-l-o!"

"There it is again!" Milo let out a low-toned whinny. It was his answer to the call.

"Milo, it's me, Chassie! Just wanted to see how you are!"

Milo spoke, "Hi, Chassie, it has been a while! Good to hear from you. How have you been?"

Chassie said, "I have been as good as can be expected, but Milo, I am thirty-three years old now. I would like to tell you about the Kentucky Derby. It is a famous horse race the humans have every year. It is a beautiful event! Horses race for a mile and a quarter."

Milo said, "Is that all?" I am just getting warmed up in a mile and a quarter!"

Chassie said, "Yes, Milo, but you are not a horse from the world! You see, Milo, you are the only horse I know that can run as fast as the wind can blow. There might be another horse that can do this, but I have not found him. Milo, you should go to Kentucky and race in the derby."

Milo said, "Sounds like fun!"

Chassie said, "It will take some supernatural help to get you into the race, but the Holy Cow will pull it off! Head for Kentucky, Milo. I will talk to you when you get there."

Milo looked at the fairies and Raven. "Well, gang, we are going to Kentucky! Find a portal into the world!"

## CHAPTER 11 | **NORTH DAKOTA**

Raven flew ahead. His nose picked up on a strange smell. It did not smell good at all! He flew back to Milo. "There is a portal just over the hill but, boy, does it smell!"

Milo said, "Do you think it will be safe to look?"

The fairies said, "It will be okay."

They trotted up to where Raven was standing. The fairies put the blanket up, and Milo stuck his head through the hole. He could not believe what he saw. Towers all over! Some had flames coming out of the tops! There was an unhealthy smell in the air. It made Milo's nose twitch.

The fairies said, "Okay, Milo, pull your head out of the hole."

Milo pulled his head out and sneezed, saying, "I will call Chassie. She will probably know what part of the world this is. Chassie! Chassie!"

"Yes, Milo, what can I do for you?"

"Chassie, we just looked through a portal into the world. There were towers and some of the towers had flames coming out of the tops, and the air STUNK!"

Chassie said, "It's North Dakota! Use the portal and head south. Follow the Missouri River south. I will let you know when you get to Missouri. Then Kentucky is east just a short distance."

Milo said, "We have to find the Missouri River." He sniffed the air. He thought he could smell the faint scent of water. He continued, "I think we are on the right course."

Raven scanned the horizon. He picked up a faint glitter. He swooped down and said, "There is water dead ahead!"

The fairies said, "It has GOT to be the Missouri River."

Milo walked along at a brisk pace. (That Milo could really cover ground at a fast walk!) Milo began to sing a horse song as he walked. His voice was beautiful.

The fairies said, "Milo, it is time to rest." They pulled the *Blanket of Sparkling Mist* over Milo and went to sleep.

Milo had a dream! In his dream, a light of peacefulness surrounded him. The light made him feel humble. Milo bowed his head and from out of the light came a voice, it was soft and beautiful. "Milo, you have been chosen by ME to change the world."

"Up until this time, you have never touched a human, and a human has never touched you, some humans will touch you. Some humans will not. Some humans will let you touch them with your nose and some will not. Remember how you touched Mhilo with your nose, and he became your brother? When you touch the humans you meet, they will become full of the virtues.

"When these humans touch each other faith, hope, love, and charity, and love will spread through the world. Milo, do this and our goal will be accomplished. Milo, you are the beginning of a revolution."

Milo awoke and suddenly his brown eyes were wide open—they had a look of joy in them. Milo woke the fairies up and told them about his dream.

The fairies said, "Milo, today we will start a revolution!"

Milo looked across the hills. He had seen some humans standing by an oil rig. They waved their arms at Milo. Milo turned and walked toward them. The men seemed glad to see a Paint Horse. Milo walked up to them. The oilmen touched Milo.

One man stood back. He had a stern look on his face. He hollered out, "You men get back to work!" Milo walked over to him and touched him with his nose. A feeling of brotherhood came over the man. He was never the same again!

Milo turned and walked away from the men and the oilrig. The men laughed. The man that Milo touched with his nose laughed. A feeling of happiness came over all of them.

Milo stopped at many oilrigs that day. The men that worked the oilrigs began talking about the horse they had seen, a Paint Horse with a raven flying overhead.

They said, "You maybe won't believe this, but the horse was singing!" The oilmen laughed.

Then one man said, "I looked at the horse through the binoculars and, I swear, he was singing!"

And so the legend of the Singing Paint Horse spread through the oil fields.

Milo reached the Missouri River.

The fairies said, "We will rest." They pulled the *Blanket of Sparkling Mist* over Milo, and they all slept.

No one had any dreams that night. They slept soundly.

When morning came, the fairies awoke first. There was Milo, standing there sleeping. They looked at his tan-colored head. It was shaped nicely. His brown eyes were just small slits. His ears were pointed forward. The Arch Fairies stood at attention by each ear.

The fairies thought about how Milo was such a kind horse. It was no wonder the Holy Cow had chosen him to live forever.

Milo's body was very muscular. His leg bones matched the size of his body, not too big and not too small. Milo was a masterpiece!

The fairies woke Milo.

Milo stretched and yawned, "Well, fairies, we better get going."

Milo, Raven, and the fairies traveled along. Milo looked up in the air and said, "Raven! Fairies! Look at the big bird! It has a very large wingspan!"

Raven said, "I will fly up and talk to him." Raven flew up to the bird. It was a big Turkey Vulture. He was gliding on the wind currents.

Raven said, "Hey, Vulture, what are you looking for?"

Vulture said, "I have been watching that Paint Horse. You know, horses have delicious eyeballs! If he drops dead, I will have choice pickings. Heh, heh, heh."

Raven said, "Milo is destined to live forever."

Vulture said, "Oh, darn! Hey, Raven! Where are you headed?"

Raven said, "We are going to Kentucky."

Vulture asked, "Can I come along?

Raven said, "Yea, come on down and meet Milo and the fairies." They flew down to Milo. Raven continued, "Vulture, this is Milo. Milo, this is Vulture."

Vulture said, "Glad to meet you, Milo."

And Milo said, "Glad to meet you, Vulture."

Vulture said, "Milo, I sure do like the looks of your eyes. Heh, heh, heh."

Milo said, "I bet you do!"

Vulture said, "You fairies look like tasty little tidbits."

Mika and Joan grabbed Vulture and twisted his neck until it almost broke!

Vulture coughed out the words, "I AM SORRY! I AM SORRY!"

Mika and Joan released their hold.

Milo laughed and said, "You are messing with the wrong gang, Vulture. Now it's time to straighten up and mind your manners."

Vulture said, "I have a hard time with associating everything I see as food. It is in my genes. If you let me go with you, you will find me to be quite valuable. I am an expert at high-flying reconnaissance."

Milo said, "We have to move out." And he started to sing "My Old Kentucky Home."

Vulture joined in. His voice was surprisingly good! His voice seemed to harmonize with Milo's voice.

Milo said, "So you want to go to Kentucky with us?"

Vulture said, "Yes, Milo! Please let me come with you!"

Milo said, "Okay, you're in!"

Vulture said, "Milo, I have got something to tell you."

Milo said, "What's that?"

"Milo, when I go by turkey farms, I stop and let the turkeys out."

Milo laughed, "Well, Vulture, there's two ways to look at that. You know the turkeys will be happy and the farmers will be sad. But you know, Vulture, the farmer and his family depend on his turkey farm to make a living. You must think about that! The farmer and his wife and family could not survive without the turkeys.

"Turkey meat is good for humans. Farmers in the world work hard to feed the world, so we must not interfere with their livelihood. If we did not have farmers, the humans in the world would not survive. Vulture, the farmers are the BEST of the BEST."

Vulture said, "I will never let the farmers' turkeys out again." Milo touched Vulture with his nose, and they became brothers. Milo walked through the rows of corn and soybeans, and the fields of wheat, hay, alfalfa, and clover. Milo came to a field of beef cattle. He jumped the fence and walked along.

A human and a horse came riding towards him twirling a rope with a loop on the end, trying to rope Milo.

Milo sidestepped, and the rope missed. Milo ran right at the human and the horse and jumped right over them. The roper tried several times to rope Milo. Milo was too quick for him, and he finally gave up. Milo walked slowly toward the human and the horse. He touched both of them with his nose, and the feeling of brotherhood swept over them. Milo turned and walked away. Milo walked across the field toward the cows. He walked amongst them. They were busy eating. They hardly noticed him. Then Milo heard a soft "moo." Milo responded to the "moo" with a whinny.

The cow spoke, "Hi, Milo. Come to change the world, did you?"

"Yes, I did, Cow," and he reached out and touched the cow with his nose.

Cow laughed and said, "Oh, Milo, the virtues are the BEST of the BEST. Milo, I have been chosen by the Holy Cow to live forever. I will help you change the world. Now go, Milo, and continue to spread the word."

Milo trotted off. He jumped the fence and headed for Nebraska. As Milo trotted along, he thought about the race. The horses that race in the Kentucky Derby were the BEST of the BEST. Milo thought about Bravo. He remembered what Bravo said about racing. Milo decided that he would not do anything to hurt the other horses' feelings. He would not race with them. *I must make my run alone.* He would talk his decision over with the fairies, Raven, and Vulture.

So Milo talked to them about the race. Raven and the fairies agreed. Vulture didn't. Vulture said, "Oh, Milo, just think about how great it would be to give those smug Thoroughbreds a good whipping!" And he laughed, "Heh, heh, heh!"

Milo said, "Vulture, I do respect your opinion on the subject, but I do not have it in my heart to do that to them."

Vulture said, "Milo, you are the BEST of the BEST!" And he flew off on the wind currents.
Milo continued on his journey to Nebraska, Kansas, Missouri, and Kentucky, touching people along the way. They were great states! Milo was impressed with all the states he traveled through.

Milo loved touching the people he met. He said, "I really like humans, but I feel sorry for them because they only have two legs, and they are so fragile."

Vulture came flying in. "Milo! Milo, I have located the race track!"

Milo said, "Lead the way!" The track was beautiful. "I bet the people of Kentucky are really proud of this place!"

Milo, Raven, Vulture, and the fairies walked into the stables.

## CHAPTER 12 | **THE KENTUCKY DERBY**

The racehorses were in their stalls. Milo touched every horse with his nose. (And I bet you know what happened! Yes! Brotherhood came over them.

The racehorses were beautiful. They were all masterpieces. It made Milo proud to be a horse. There was an empty stall at the end. Milo stepped into the stall, and the fairies closed the gate. Raven and Vulture said, "We will roost on top of the grandstand." The fairies pulled the *Blanket of Sparkling Mist* over Milo and went to sleep.

Vulture and Raven looked up in the sky. The stars and the moon were very bright. Vulture said, "Raven, tomorrow the world will witness the unbelievable!"

Raven said, "Yes, they will see Milo run as fast as the wind can blow. It will be the BEST of the BEST!" (How fast do you think the wind can blow?)

Milo slept soundly that night. He did not dream. He awoke early, stood up and looked around. The stables were busy. The trainers were getting the horses ready for the race and they did not notice Milo in the end stall. The fairies opened the gate. Milo walked through the hustle and bustle. No one noticed him. Milo walked toward the track. He walked out onto the track. The surface was beautiful. Milo thought *I should be able to put down a great time!*

Milo walked toward the starting gate; all the other racehorses were still in their stalls. People in the grandstands started to notice Milo. Some oilmen from North Dakota said, "Hey, that's the Paint Horse we saw in the oil fields!"

Ranchers and farmers recognized Milo. The cattlemen from South Dakota said, "That's the horse I tried to rope!"

People from North Dakota, South Dakota, Kansas, Nebraska, Missouri, and Kentucky all said, "That's the Paint Horse that touched us with his nose!"

The crowd began to quiet down as they noticed Milo. Milo walked up to the starting gate and stepped in. Raven tripped the gate. Milo came out of the gate with a mighty lunge. The crowd roared! Milo broke into an eighty mile per hour gallop. His mane and tail waved in the wind. It wasn't long, and Milo had rounded the track and was heading toward the starting gate.

Raven was sitting on top of the gate. When Milo reached a precise point, Raven hollered, "Jump up!" (If you were wondering where Mika and Joan were when Milo made his run, they were sitting on top of the starting gate in case Milo didn't make his jump.) "Watch out, now. Here comes Milo!"

Milo jumped, and he cleared the gate by four feet. He was now approaching the finish line; he stopped three feet short, took a bow, and stepped across. Milo had averaged eighty miles per hour for the full run. Milo broke into a trot and went around the track one more time.

The crowd roared again.

Vulture swooped down and grabbed the microphone out of the announcer's hand. "Folks," he said, "You ain't seen nothing yet!" Then he handed the microphone back to the announcer and flew away.

After the other horses ran the actual race, the trainers noticed a glow coming from the stall on the end. They all walked down to the stall. One trainer opened the gate and there, written on the wall in sparkling glitter, were the words:

OWNER: HOLY COW
TRAINERS: FAITH, HOPE, LOVE, CHARITY, MIKA, JOAN
HORSE'S NAME: MILO, QUARTER HORSE, BUCKSKIN PAINT
PLACE OF ORIGIN: THE SPECIAL PLACE

The trainers stepped forward, one at a time. They touched the sparkling glitter and it stuck to their fingers. The virtues swept over them.  Milo walked around, but the people didn't seem to notice him. Their attention was all on the announcer and the owners and the jockey that had ridden the winner.  The winning horse stood in the background. He had a huge wreath of roses around his neck. Milo walked up to him and touched the horse with his nose. A feeling of brotherhood swept over them.

Thoroughbred said, "What's your name?"

"Milo is my name."

Thoroughbred said, "Most of the horses know all about you, Milo!"

Milo said, "How's that?"

"The horse Chassie from Minnesota talks to us. She said you would be coming to Kentucky."

Milo said, "Well, Thoroughbred, you have won one race now! Two more and you will win the Triple Crown!"

Thoroughbred said, "I sure hope so!"

Milo said, "No 'hoping'! Think positive! You will be a true champion!"

Milo touched Thoroughbred with his nose one more time. The *Blanket of Sparkling Mist* descended over them, and then it disappeared.

Milo walked away—he had a smile on his face. Thoroughbred WOULD win the Triple Crown!

The fairies, Raven, and Vulture all met up with Milo.

"Well," Milo said, "it's time to move out," and Milo took off at a trot.

They traveled across the country. It was beautiful. The night was dark. Milo and the fairies walked along.   Vulture and Raven were sleeping on Milo's back.

The fairies looked up at the stars in the sky. They said, "Milo, look up!"

Milo said, "What do you mean?"

The fairies said, "Put your head back. Look up!"

Milo stopped walking. He had never looked up before at night! He said, "Holy Cow! This is unreal!"

"They are stars, Milo!" The stars glittered in the sky. "Make a wish on the stars, Milo."

"What do you mean?" Milo asked.

"Think of something that you really want to happen, wish for it. Do not tell us what your wish is or it will not happen."

So Milo wished and two small tears formed in his beautiful brown eyes. Milo thought, *PEACE! Peace in the world.*

And he bowed his head.

The fairies tried to read Milo's mind, but they could not. (The Holy Cow had taken that power away from them, so Milo's wish could come true. There COULD be peace and brotherhood in the world!)

All of a sudden, the fairies noticed that the moon was coming up. It was a full moon.

Milo said, "It is beautiful! Can you wish on the moon?"

"Yes, Milo," the fairies said.

"Hey, Milo," Raven said. "Hey diddle diddle, the cat and the fiddle, the cow jumped over the moon. The little dog laughed to see such sport, and the dish ran away with the spoon."

Milo laughed, "Oh, Raven, that was the BEST of the BEST!" Milo thought, *My companions are the BEST of the BEST!*   He thanked the Holy Cow for their friendship.

The moonlight lit up the night. It was soft and it made Milo's soul feel good!

The fairies said, "Milo, look at our shadows!" The fairies flew around. Their shadows darted across the ground.

Milo laughed, and he looked at his shadow. "Fairies, look at my shadow!"

Their shadows darted around Milo's shadow. Milo stood on his hind legs, and his shadow was magnificent! Milo bucked, trotted, galloped and his shadow stayed right with him!

Raven and Vulture sat in a tree and watched. The fairies did all kinds of flying tricks, and their shadows stayed right with them too. What great copycats those shadows were! The moon rose higher in the sky, and the shadows became smaller.

Milo said, "Look! My shadow is the same size as me!" The fairies laughed. Milo continued, "I wonder if I can outrun my shadow?" Milo trotted to the far end of the field... he turned around and looked.

He saw that the edge of the field was one-quarter mile away. His shadow stood alongside him. The field had a huge oak tree at the end of the quarter mile. Milo knew he must be able to stop before he got to the trees.

Milo took off like a rocket! His speed was ninety-two miles per hour. His shadow stayed right with him. *I better not run any faster or I won't be able to stop before I get to the trees!* It was time to stop!

Milo set his front and hind legs down. He slid across the grass. It was slippery because of the night dew. Closer and closer he got to the trees. The huge oak tree was straight ahead. Milo slid up to the oak tree, and his nose touched it as he came to a stop. The bark on the oak tree began to sparkle because Milo had touched it with his nose. The sparkling worked its way up the tree trunk and then all the leaves lit up! The oak tree was beautiful in the night. Milo bowed his head, and the shadow bowed its head. It was a very moving experience for Milo.

Milo said, "Shadow, you can run as fast as I can. Congratulations!" Milo let out a huge whinny, and his shadow let out a huge whinny. The two whinnies echoed across the moonlit night.

Milo looked at the shadow and said, "I didn't know you could make a sound!"

The shadow said, "I didn't know that YOU could make a sound!"

Milo said, "It sure is a beautiful night! I will race you back to the fairies!"

The shadow said, "It is a beautiful night. I will race YOU back to the fairies!"

Both Milo and the shadow laughed.

Milo said, "You are a copycat."

The shadow said, "YOU are a copycat."

Milo became silent. The shadow became silent.

Milo looked up. Some dark clouds covered the moon, and his shadow went away.

Milo walked back to the fairies. He said, "I am tired."

They pulled the *Blanket of Sparkling Mist* over themselves and went to sleep.

## CHAPTER 13 | **MILO MEETS BULL AND TURTLE**

When morning came, Milo opened his eyes, and there stood a huge Hereford bull looking right at him. Milo said, "Good morning, Mr. Bull!"

Mr. Bull looked right into Milo's eyes. Milo looked right into Mr. Bull's eyes.

Mr. Bull's eyes had a kind look in them. Mr. Bull spoke, "Well, well, well. Mr. Horse, what are you doing in my pasture?"

Milo stuttered. He was a little nervous. He had never talked to a Hereford bull before. "I…I was t-t-tired, so …so I thought I…I…I would s-sleep here. I am s-s-sorry."

Mr. Bull said, "Oh, don't be sorry!" He touched Milo with his nose, and a feeling of brotherhood went through Milo's body.

Milo said, "WOW! That is sure different!"

Mr. Bull said, "Yes, Milo, you are not the only one that has been chosen by the Holy Cow to do this. Hey, Milo, want to see something real neat? Come to the pond with me, and I will show you the snapping turtles."

The huge Hereford bull led Milo to the pond. The pond was four and a half acres in size. It was eight feet deep at its deepest point. Cattails lined the edge.

The bull walked up to the edge. He stomped his foot. The water began to bubble. Milo stepped back. The big bull laughed, and then from out of the deep came a big snapping turtle. She was the size of a washtub.

She swam over to Milo and Mr. Bull. She said, "Well, Mr. Bull, who is your partner?"

"My partner is Milo the horse."

She said, "Glad to meet you, Horse."

Milo said, "Glad to meet you, Turtle," and they both laughed.

Turtle said, "Hey, Horse, someday we should have a cross-country race!"

Milo laughed. "You would be no match for me, Turtle, for I can run as fast as the wind can blow!"

Turtle said, "Milo, have you ever heard the story of 'The Tortoise and the Hare'?"

Milo said, "No, I have never heard that story."

Turtle said, "Good! And I will never tell it to you," and she smiled.

*I wonder what that story is about? I better stop thinking about it. She is confusing me.*

Turtle said, "Milo, I would like you to meet my family," and she slipped under the water. Soon the whole pond began to bubble and, one at a time, the turtles came to the surface. They swam over to Milo and walked up on the land. There were thirty of them, some as big as their mother. Some were smaller.

Milo said, "This is WONDERFUL!" The fairies clapped their hands. The turtles began to laugh. Milo noticed that their laughing was beautiful.

They stopped laughing and the mother said, "Milo, we would like to sing a song for you." She started to sing, and her children joined in. What a beautiful choir they were!

It was the song from the Special Place! Milo asked the fairies, "How do they know that song?"

The fairies said, "Milo, turtles have been around since time began, since the world was formed, since the world was created."

The song brought tears to Milo's eyes. It was the BEST of the BEST!

When the song finished, Turtle said, "Milo, this is my family. We all love each other and we all swim together."

Milo, the fairies, Raven, Vulture, and Mr. Bull gave them the "Hip-Hip-Hooray!" salute.

The turtles all slipped into the water and disappeared.

Milo turned and looked at Mr. Bull. Milo said, "Thank you! This has been a very inspiring time for me! Oh, by the way, Mr. Bull, would you tell me the story about 'The Tortoise and the Hare'?"

Mr. Bull laughed and walked away.

Milo turned and looked at the fairies, Raven, and Vulture. They all laughed, too. They had promised Turtle that they would not tell Milo the story, and they would never break their promise.

(Well, well, well! Do you think that Turtle has come from the Special Place? Could Holy Cow have given her a special gift? Why did she instantly challenge Milo to a cross-country race? Who would win? WE will never know unless they meet again.)

## CHAPTER 14 | **ST. GEORGE AND THE DRAGON**

The fairies, Milo, Raven, and Vulture discussed where they would go next. It was unanimous! They would head west and look for a portal into the dimension where they had come from. They all began to sniff for fresh air.

Soon they found a portal. They covered the portal with the *Blanket of Sparkling Mist*, took a chance, and walked in without looking. The fog was so thick that Milo could hardly see four feet in front of him!

Milo said, "Do not move! We must hold completely still until the fog clears!" Just then, Milo felt a slight breeze.

"Milo, it's me, Wind. I will clear the fog. DO…NOT…MOVE." Wind increased his speed and began to push on the fog. The fog slowly moved away from Milo.

Milo looked down. He was standing on the EDGE of a PRECIPICE! If he had taken one more step, he would have fallen into an abyss—a bottomless pit!

The fairies screamed!

Milo backed away from the edge of the cliff.

Raven said, "Vulture and I will fly to the bottom."

Mika and Joan said, "We will go, too!"

So off they went, flying downward to the bottom.

Milo and the fairies waited for three hours before they heard them coming back. Mika and Joan flew out first. They were carrying a large, bleached skull.

Milo said, "What is it?"

Mika and Joan spoke together, "Dragon skull, Milo. It's a dragon skull."

Vulture flew up and lit on Milo. "The hole is a dragon burial ground. About 6,000 years ago, there were dragons in this dimension. There were good dragons and bad dragons. A human named St. George hunted the bad dragons down and ended their lives. He rode a white horse. I think the horse was a Marwari— the tips of the horse's ears touch. The horse was fifteen point two hands tall. The horse Inferno is much bigger!"

Milo said, "I know a horse named Inferno."

Vulture said, "Is he colored gray, black, and purple?"

"Yes," Milo said. "He is a wonderful horse and a great father. He and Azura have two small horses, a colt and a filly."

Vulture continued, "St. George would sever the dragons heads and throw their heads into the hole. St. George still roams this dimension. We could meet him someday. I know all about St. George. The vultures followed him around and cleaned up the mess, after he ended the bad dragons' lives.

"St. George carried a mighty sword. When he withdrew it from his scabbard, it glowed like the sun! It blinded the bad dragons. And then he could sever their heads. St. George was not a huge, muscle-bound human. His strength came from his faith, his hope, his love, and his charity.

"I will tell you where St. George came from. St. George was created by the Top Being — when I say 'Top', there is no other direction to go. The Top Being created everything from the bottom to the top, from the right to the left. He created the Holy Cow. He created nothing and he created everything. And that's where St. George came from.

"He held St. George in his hands and he set him down on the world. He taught him about the dimensions and how to go from one to the other. When the Top Being set St. George on the world, he gave him no means of transportation. So the Holy Cow said she would change this. She would give St. George a horse.

"St. George walked along dragging his sword. It did not seem to tire him. He heard a horse walking toward him. The horse stepped from behind a big tree. The horse was beautiful. His color was white. He

looked majestic. He also looked sacred. He paused and looked at St. George, and then he spoke, 'Looking for a ride, George?' He did not speak normally. He chanted.

"George stepped back. He didn't know horses could sing! George said, 'Where are you from?'"

"The horse, still chanting, said, 'The Special Place, sent by the Holy Cow. Jump on, George!' George stepped back. He took a short run and used his sword as a polevault. He was light on his feet.

"George's balance and stability were second to none. His gymnastic abilities were the BEST of the BEST. George stood atop the horse.

"Horse chanted, 'Sit down, George, and I will give you the ride of a lifetime!'

"George laughed, 'I do not have to sit down, Horse. Show me what you have got.'

"Horse thought (chanting), 'George will be lying in the dirt in a few seconds.' He reared up and took off like a shot out of a cannon. But George did not fall off. He rode Horse standing. George withdrew his sword. The light from the sword did not blind Horse. The Holy Cow had given Horse a special set of eyelids so the sun-sword did not blind him. George swung the sword over his head. He did every trick that a majorette could do with a baton.

"Horse slowed and came to a stop. Horse said, still chanting, 'George, how did you learn to do what you just did?'

"George said, 'The Top Being gave this gift to me. I did not learn it, and He christened me St. George! And now, Horse, I will christen you.'

"St. George laid his sword between Horse's ears. Horse knelt. George spoke, his voice echoing across the countryside, 'By the power given to me by the Top Being, I do christen you! Your name will be JUSTICE! JUSTICE! JUSTICE!'

"The name echoed across the countryside.

"George said, 'Justice, I will command you with my thoughts when we go into battle. Our minds will become one. Justice, we are the BEST of the BEST, created by the Top Being and the Holy Cow. Don't ever forget this! Our motto will be…humbly triumphant!'"

Vulture bowed his head and then he took off. He circled higher and higher. He hollered out, "Going to look for St. George. I will be back someday." And he disappeared into the clear, blue sky.

Milo said, "What a great bird Vulture is! I totally misjudged Vulture when I first met him. I must be careful not to judge too quickly. I will miss him very much."

Milo, the fairies, and Raven took a moment of silence.

## CHAPTER 15 | **MILO AND INFERNO MEET AGAIN**

Raven said, "We should move out!" The landscape was full of deep canyons but there was a path. It had hoof prints of a very large horse on it.

Milo said, "These hoof prints are either prints from St. George's horse, or maybe Inferno is in this area."

The path through the canyons opened up into a rolling plain. You could see for miles. Milo stopped on top of a rise. There was sagebrush and a few junipers scattered across the plain.

The fairies said, "It is unusual to see junipers and sagebrush in this dimension."

Milo scanned the horizon and far off in the distance there was a cloud of dust rising from the ground. Milo thought, *I would like to know what that dust cloud is from.* He hollered out, "Fairies! Raven! Hang on! I am going to see if I can run that dust cloud down!"

Milo went into a gallop, picking up speed. He found he could run safely at eighty-five miles an hour. He ran toward the cloud of dust at eighty-five miles an hour. Milo was really gaining on it. The dust cloud was just over the rise and then it disappeared.

Whatever it was, it stopped.

All of a sudden, a big horse stepped in front of Milo. Milo jumped right over the horse and came to a stop. He spun around and there stood Inferno!

Inferno spoke, "Just testing your reflexes, Milo!"

Milo was speechless! His whole body shook! A feeling of rage entered his body, "Inferno, you could have killed us both!"

Inferno said, "Milo, that will never happen because the Holy Cow has destined us to live forever."

Milo calmed down. He looked at Inferno and started to laugh.

Inferno laughed, too. Inferno said, "It is so good to see you, Milo."

"Likewise, Inferno, but I am very tired. I am ready to sleep. It has been a big day!"

Milo and Inferno bedded down. The fairies sat on Milo's nose. Raven sat in a juniper tree. And the *Blanket of Sparkling Mist* hovered over them.

The Holy Cow looked down on them and smiled. She thought what wonderful creations they were. Inferno woke first. He gave Milo a push, and Milo rolled over like a rolling pin. Inferno's strength was awesome! Inferno grabbed Milo with his front feet, reared up, and held Milo over his head.

Milo was laughing. Inferno set Milo down.

Milo said, "Your strength is awesome, but you cannot run as fast as the wind can blow."

Inferno said, "You got it, Milo! Now let's see if we can find St. George."

The fairies jumped on Inferno's back; Mika and Joan stood between his ears. Raven flew above, and Milo trotted behind.

Inferno's trot was as smooth as silk. The four-thousand-pound horse was a sight to behold.

Inferno could trot around the world and never tire.

Inferno's coat of gray, black, and purple glistened like fine silk.

Inferno started to sing. His baritone voice echoed across the countryside.

Milo joined in.

Milo's voice was tenor.

Their songs were the BEST of the BEST!

Milo and Inferno stopped to talk. Milo said, "Inferno, how did you survive all those wars?"

"The Holy Cow gave me some special gifts, Milo!" Inferno bowed his head. A light purple haze formed around his body. His eyes began to glitter. He continued, "Watch this, Milo," and Inferno trotted right up to a large juniper tree. He hit the tree, and it shattered into pieces.

Inferno turned and looked at Milo. Milo began to shiver. Inferno said, "You ain't seen nothing yet! Don't be afraid, for my soul is of faith, hope, love, and charity. And Milo, you are my brother forever."

Inferno stomped the ground. The ground shook like an earthquake. Inferno's voice echoed across the dimension, "FOREVER...FOREVER...FOREVER!"

Milo and Inferno bowed their heads.

Then Milo looked at Inferno, saying, "Where are Azura and the little ones?"

Inferno said, "Azura took the little tykes to see the farmlands."

Milo said, "There are farmlands in this dimension?"

"Oh, yes, Milo, the richest farmlands since time began! The Top Being put the Holy Cow in charge of the farmlands. She raised all the food crops and all the fruit crops that exist in the world. Nothing has been genetically altered. Everything is pure and clean."

Milo said, "What does she do with all that food?"

"The Holy Cow feeds everyone and everything that lives in the Special Place and in the other dimensions. Lots of us do not have to eat; but believe me, Milo, when you taste her food, you will love it. No one starves in the Special Place or in the other dimensions. Remember the bee you met in the huge flower patch? She does all the pollinating. The Holy Cow says she is the 'Gift of Life.'"

Milo said, "What about the world?"

"The Top Being said the world is on its own. He put humans on the world who are supposed to be smart enough to figure the food thing out! They have failed since time began. Humans starve all over the world."

Milo said, "Yes, humans are a strange thing and they only have two legs...and they are fragile."

Inferno said, "And, Milo, they pay farmers not to raise crops. They like to see their fellow humans starve."

Milo said, "This is strange for me to comprehend! I don't get it! They have to change their ways! They must live by the virtues of faith, hope, love, and charity!!!" Their voices echoed throughout the dimension.

Inferno said, "They raise corn to make fuel for their automobiles, so they can go nowhere fast and run over things that get in their way."

Milo said, "How do they justify this when humans are starving in the world?"

Inferno said, "Humans are weird! They can justify just about everything, whatever suits them."

Milo shook his head and said, "Well, we better get on our way."

Inferno and Milo broke into a gallop. They headed for the farmlands to see Azura and the little tykes.

Milo's ears picked up on a voice calling. It was Chassie. Inferno heard her voice, too, and Milo came to a halt.

Chassie spoke, "Milo and Inferno, I made it to the Special Place."

Milo said, "Oh, how wonderful!"

Inferno said, "Likewise!"

Chassie continued, "Oh, you guys, it is beautiful here. I met the Holy Cow and I drank her milk and I became young again! I can run and jump and rear up! It is the BEST of the BEST!"

Inferno and Milo cheered, and they gave Chassie the "Hip-Hip-Hooray!" salute.

There was no sadness that Chassie had left the world.

The fairies flew around and cheered. Raven did cartwheels in the air. Milo began to sing. Inferno and the fairies joined in. It was the song from the Special Place. It was beautiful!

Tears of joy rolled down Chassie's cheeks. She had achieved the ultimate. It was the BEST of the BEST! Everyone became silent.

Milo had a big smile on his face and then he began to laugh, and everyone began to laugh. Laughing, smiling, happiness, joy, brotherhood, faith, hope, love, and charity....

It is the BEST of the BEST!

The fairies hollered out, "Let's move out!" and they continued on their journey.

Milo and Inferno trotted up a short rise in the terrain. When they reached the top, there were the farmlands in all their glory.

Wind came drifting by. "Hi, Milo, just helping with the pollinating," and he laughed and drifted away.

Azura and the little tykes came running in. They ran up to their father and touched him. Azura walked up to Inferno and touched his nose and gave a low-toned whinny. Inferno acknowledged it with his own low-toned whinny. The feeling of love radiated from the family.

Milo bowed his head. *Thank you, Holy Cow, for this day!*

## CHAPTER 16 | **MILO LOOKS FOR ST. GEORGE**

The fairies said, "Milo, we must go look for St. George."

Milo walked over to Inferno and said his goodbyes. Both horses reared up and smacked their hooves together, and then Milo trotted away.

Milo, the fairies, and Raven headed northwest. They were headed for a mountain range (not the mountains that got 250 degrees below zero). They stepped out onto a desert floor. It was smooth and not too hard and not too soft.

Milo thought this was a place where he could really turn it on. Milo broke into a gallop, and all the fairies hid under his mane. "Do not try to ride on me, Raven!"

Milo's speed soon was 100 miles per hour. His muscles felt good as he limbered up, and then he turned it on. Milo was running at 300 miles per hour…with ease!

The mountains appeared on the horizon. *I better slow down.* Milo began to slow down. Soon he was at eighty miles per hour, then seventy…sixty…forty…twenty…and then he came to a stop.

The fairies crawled out of Milo's mane and said, "Milo, you are nuts!"

Milo said, "No, I am a horse. My name is Milo and I can run faster than the wind can blow. Remember, the Holy Cow made me this way," and he began to laugh.

Milo laughed so hard, he had to lie down. The fairies covered him with the *Blanket of Sparkling Mist.* Milo said, "Raven will be here in the morning," and he went to sleep.

When Milo awoke, he jumped up. He felt a little stiff from that 300 miles per hour run he had done the day before. He stretched and trotted around and soon he was loosened up. He looked at the mountain range. He had a gut feeling that St. George lived in the mountains. (Most of the time, Milo's gut feelings were right. Gut feelings come with age.)

Raven came flying in, "Milo, you are crazy!"

"Oh, Raven, not as bad as you!" And they began to laugh.

The fairies put their heads together and began to hum. They stopped, looked at Milo, and they all spoke at once. "St. George lives in the mountains, these mountains, Milo. Let's go!" They jumped on Milo's back.

Soon, Milo was at the base of the mountains. He stopped, turned his ears toward the mountains, and listened. He could hear a horse's footsteps. Milo didn't know what direction they came from. The sound echoed through the mountains.

Milo started to climb. Up and down he went. He smelled the air. He could smell a horse. He stepped out on a small flat and stopped. From the far end of the flat, a horse came at a full gallop. There was a human standing on his back. He carried a large sword. He twirled the sword in the air. He and the horse came running in and stopped.

The human did a double back flip off the horse and landed in front of Milo. He spoke, "St. George at your service."

Milo spoke, "It's a pleasure to meet you, George. My name is Milo."

George spoke, "Yeah, I heard about you. I talked to Chassie. Hey, did you hear she went to the Special Place?"

Milo said, "Yes, I did."

George said, "Hey, Milo, have you seen any dragons lately?"

"No, George, I haven't."

George said, "Aw, gee!"

George's horse stayed at attention, he did not move. The horse was white. He was spotlessly clean.

George said, "Justice, come over here."

Justice walked over to Milo. Justice chanted, "Hello, Milo, it is a pleasure to meet you."

Milo took a bow. *Does Justice always speak this way?*

Justice chanted, "Milo, fairies, Raven, I know all about you. It is a wonderful thing that you are doing."

"Thank you," Milo said, and the fairies said likewise.

Raven said, "Your chanting is beautiful."

"Thank you, Raven, the Holy Cow made me this way. This is how I always speak."

George said, "Justice is a sacred horse," and Justice took a bow.

Justice's ears touched together at the tips. Milo said, "You are a Marwari! This is the first time I have ever seen a Marwari Horse."

Justice chanted, "Yes, Milo, we are a very special breed."

George spoke, "Justice is the BEST of the BEST!" George threw his sword into the air. When it came down, it just about touched the ground, and Justice gave the sword a kick. It headed straight for George! George caught the sword handle first, swung it above his head, and placed it tip first in the ground.

Everyone was amazed!

Justice chanted, "George and I are a team. Teamwork is what makes us so successful. Milo, the fairies, and Raven are a team. That is why they do so well. If humans lived by the virtues and practiced teamwork, there would be peace throughout the world. I truly feel sorry for humans, they only have two legs and they are very fragile. And then there are the One Percent…NO COMMENT!"

George, Justice, Milo, the fairies, and Raven knelt down. A huge black cloud formed above them. A lightning bolt came from the cloud, hit the ground, and blew a hole in the ground eight feet in diameter and four feet deep.

A voice came out of the cloud—it was the voice of the Top Being, "Keep up the work. If the humans do not change their ways, I will take the matter into my own hands…and it won't be pretty!"

The cloud disappeared, everyone looked up, and there was Vulture circling. Vulture swooped down and everyone greeted him.

The fairies said, "Vulture, did you just see what happened?"

"Yes, I thought the Top Being took you guys out, and then I was going to clean up the mess. Heh, heh, heh!" Vulture looked at Milo. " You sure have got beautiful eyes."

Everyone scowled at Vulture.

Vulture said, "Just kidding!" He laughed. No one else laughed.

Milo said, "It is so good to see you again, Vulture. You always seem to make things interesting." Milo reached out with his front foot. He laid his hoof on top of Vulture's head and said, "My friend forever, believe it or not."

Tears formed in Vulture's eyes. Vulture said, "Milo, you are my brother."

Everyone hollered out, "Hip-Hip-Hooray!"

Justice walked over to Milo and Vulture. Justice chanted, "Vulture, you are a wonderful bird. Vultures have practiced brotherhood from the time they were created. I respect you all for this."

Vulture said, "Thank you, Justice, I sure do appreciate that comment!" He roughed his feathers, spread his wings, and looked beautiful (hard to believe that a vulture could look beautiful!).

Everyone looked at Vulture in awe. He WAS magnificent!

Justice chanted, "The reason Vulture looks so beautiful to you all is you have taken everything into account—his sense of humor, his flying ability, his usefulness in nature, and his ability to practice brotherhood from the time he was created. Beauty is only skin deep. You must look past the outer surface. Amen!"

## CHAPTER 17 | **THE MUSIC DIMENSION**

The fairies spoke up, "Milo, we must move on. We must find a portal into the world. We have got a lot of work to do." They said, "Anyone that wants to come with us can."

Everyone said, "We will come with you and help you find a portal." They all started out. Justice and George led the way. Justice and George were leaders. They instantly took command of the team. The team walked swiftly along. Justice was a real mover. Milo walked by his side. George was a quiet human; he never had much to say. Raven and Vulture flew on high. The fairies flew ahead. They heard a strange sound. They flew around the sound area.

Justice walked up. He chanted, "It is the Music Dimension! We must enter this dimension." George took his sword, held it high, and the door opened to the dimension. Justice, Milo and the team walked in. There was a faint yellow haze in the air. A song drifted in. It was a perfect song that welcomed everyone. It was a song that wiped all apprehension from the team's bodies and minds. The song finished and drifted away.

Milo spoke, "Let's enter into the land of music."

They walked along. Instruments floated by. They played beautiful music. Each one played a complete song and drifted away. A feeling of serenity came over everyone.

Musical notes appeared in the yellow haze. They unscrambled themselves and formed into lines, then words formed under them, and then a voice began to sing the words. It was a voice of a woman. It was unbelievably beautiful!

When the song finished, Milo said, "Holy Cow! Where did that voice come from?"

Raven said, "The song and the voice came from the world you see, Milo. The Top Being created the woman, the voice, the song, and the music. There is no one else that can sing like that."

Milo was amazed.

Justice chanted, "The woman's name is Barbra."

The team moved through the dimension, and the music and the songs continued. There were no songs of death, drugs, killings, or impurities. There were no songs of racism or war.

The songs were of faith, hope, love, and charity—songs of brotherhood. The songs cleansed your soul and purified your mind. The songs made you laugh and made you sing and made you cry tears of joy.

It was the most beautiful thing that Milo had ever witnessed. Milo stood in silence. *MUSIC is the BEST of the BEST!*

"Milo, Milo, M-i-l-o."

Milo spoke, "Yes, Chassie?"

"Milo, I am from the state of Minnesota. Minnesota has the best symphony orchestra in the world, and I am very proud of all the people in it."

Milo spoke, "Oh, Chassie, you have such a wonderful mind!"

Milo spoke again, "We will have to leave this dimension of music."

George lifted his sword high and the team walked into their dimension.

## CHAPTER 18 | **COMPETITION**

Everyone was tired. They bedded down under the *Blanket of Sparkling Mist* and slept.

Milo dreamed that night. A voice came into his head. It was the voice of the Holy Cow. "Milo, a lot of humans and horses laugh at your achievements. They say the Kentucky thing was some sort of a trick. The super horses and the performance horses think you are a wimp because you practice faith, love, hope, charity, and brotherhood.

"Well, Milo, I am very competitive when my creation is scoffed at. I am ready to prove them wrong. I am going to add competitiveness to your mind. You will love it! We will set aside your kindness for now. You will want to win at everything you do. No second places. You will go into the world and you will do some big-time butt kicking! Look out, super horses and performance horses, here comes Milo!"

The Holy Cow said, "The blood that flows in your veins is pure horse blood. There is not a little bit of this and a little bit of that. Your blood was created by me. You are a beautiful Buckskin Paint because I like Buckskin Paints.

"The message in Kentucky that was painted on the wall said, 'Quarter Horse.' If I would have called you 'One Quarter Faith, One Quarter Hope, One Quarter Love, One Quarter Charity Horse,' no one in the world would understand. That is why I called you a Quarter Horse. Milo, you are one of a kind. There is no other horse like you. Your goal to win will come first, kindness will come later."

Milo awoke. He jumped up. *What a dream!*

The fairies flew around him. They spoke, "What do you think, Milo? Are you ready for the challenge?"

Milo spoke, "You bet I am! Bring it on! When I get done with the horses in the world, they will know that the horse named Milo is no wimp!" Milo said, "Let's find a portal into the world."

George said, "Justice and I must move along," and Justice galloped away.

The fairies, Vulture, and Raven flew ahead. Soon they found a portal. They put the *Blanket of Sparkling Mist* over the portal, and Milo stuck his head through. It was the world.

Milo spoke, "Let's go in."

They stepped into a small patch of trees. They looked through the trees. They were looking at a horse arena, pipe fences, and gates.

Raven said, "This is a competition place for horses."

There were no humans or horses there yet. They heard the rumble of a straight-piped 5.9 Cummins coming. An old Dodge pickup came driving in; it was pulling a four-place horse trailer. It was gray in color. The pickup stopped. A young girl jumped out. She walked over to the arena. No one was there, yet she walked inside.

The fairies said, "The trailer is empty."

Milo walked over to the trailer. The fairies opened the doors, and Milo stepped in. Raven sat on top of the trailer. The girl came out of the arena. She walked toward the truck. She noticed Raven sitting on the trailer. She thought, *That sure is unusual.* She touched the door handle on the pickup.

Milo spoke, "Jessica."

Jessica spun around. No one was there. *I must be hearing things.*

Milo spoke. "Jessica."

Jessica got a fearful look on her face.

Milo spoke, "Do not be afraid. Look in the trailer."

Jessica peeked in the trailer.

There stood a Buckskin Paint!

Jessica's heart began to race.

She thought, *I think I am going to faint!*

Milo spoke, "Come in the trailer, I want to talk to you."

Jessica walked into the trailer. She touched Milo on the butt as she walked alongside him.

Milo spoke, "Scratch right there. I am itchy."

Jessica laughed, Milo spoke, "Jessica, you have been chosen by the Holy Cow to ride me." He told her what the mission was about. Milo put his nose on her face, and the warm air on her face felt mystical.

A feeling of complete confidence came over Jessica. She WOULD ride Milo. *Bring it on world!*

Jessica's mind was in a whirl, but then reality kicked in. *How will I be able to afford this?*

Then Raven spoke, and Jessica was startled. *This is unreal—a horse and a raven talking!*

"Jessica, you will be able to afford this. The hay bags will always be full, the water pails will always be full, and the glove box in the old pickup will always have money in it. Trust us. The old pickup will never break down, so put your mind at ease. Oh, Jessica, I forgot to tell you. Milo does not have to eat or drink. We have to have water and hay so we look legitimate. Milo can eat or drink if he wants."

The people started to drive in. Their rigs were beautiful, they glittered in the sunlight. They unloaded their horses.

Milo had never seen so many horses. They were all beautiful. Milo was so glad he was a horse! *And, boy, am I glad I have got four legs!*

Jessica had come to the competition to look at a horse she was thinking about buying. The horse was a Quarter Horse with a touch of Arabian in her blood. She was beautiful. Jessica thought, *I cannot buy this horse because I made a commitment to Milo. He will need my attention, and I will need his.*

Jessica did not buy the horse. The horse won all the competitions that day. She was one of a kind!

Milo thought, *That horse will be a super horse someday, and I will compete against her.*

Milo got a big grin on his face.

Jessica had watched the competition that day. *I hope Milo knows what he is in for!* She did not know about Milo's lightning reflexes or how he could run faster than the wind could blow. She did not know about Milo's internal timer.

Milo hoped Jessica's riding ability was second-to-none, because if she was going to stay on him, she would have to be at the top of her game. If she got in trouble, he would be able to keep her in balance, but he did not like to do that any more than he had to; it could throw him off a little.

Milo said, "Jessica, come over here. We must head for our first super-horse competition. Jessica, the fairies will tell you where to go."

Jessica said, "Fairies?"

Milo spoke, "Oh, I forgot to tell you about the six fairies. They are guardians." Milo said, "Get ready, Jessica, here they come!" The fairies flew out of Milo's mane. They flew around Jessica. They each gave off a different glow.

Jessica was awestruck—she could not speak.

Milo said, "Jessica, I will introduce you to the fairies." So Milo introduced Jessica to the six fairies.

They flew in front of Jessica one at a time. After Milo introduced each one, they kissed Jessica on the cheek. Then they flew back to Milo.

Jessica said, "This is the BEST of the BEST!"

Milo said, "Jessica, look at yourself in the pickup mirror."

Jessica looked in the mirror and there, on her cheek, was a small tattoo of a fairy. Jessica reached up and touched the tattoo and it disappeared!

Jessica was amazed! She touched the back of her hand and it appeared. She couldn't believe her eyes. She touched the tattoo and it disappeared! She touched her arm and it appeared! Jessica did not like to have tattoos on her body. She didn't care if other people had tattoos, many of her friends did. So Jessica touched the tattoo on her arm and it disappeared.

Jessica thought, *I wonder if I touch my shirt, the fairies will appear!* So Jessica touched her right shoulder and two fairies appeared on her shirt. She then touched her left shoulder and two more fairies appeared on the shirt. Jessica then touched her collar's right side and left side and the two Arch Fairies appeared on the collar.

Jessica loved what she saw! (What Jessica did not know was that the shirt would also never get dirty, and the shirt would change colors—whatever color she would like.)

Milo said, "We must go."

Jessica jumped into the old Dodge truck and away they went.

The Arch Fairies sat on Jessica's shoulders; they would tell her where to go. Everyone else rode in the trailer with Milo. The day was beautiful.

The Arch Fairies spoke, "Jessica, look ahead!" High in the sky flew Vulture. "That bird is one of us."

Jessica spoke, "Do you mean he is part of the team? "

"Yes, he is, and he can speak your language."

Jessica laughed and hollered out, "This is nuts!"

The Arch Fairies laughed and said, "Jessica, pull into the next rest stop. We will introduce you to the one and only Vulture."

The Arch Fairies spoke, "Rest stop coming up!"

Jessica pulled in. She let Milo out of the trailer. Milo walked around and stretched. He began to sing a quiet little horse song.

Jessica was amazed.

Vulture came flying in and lit right in front of Jessica. Vulture spoke, "It is a pleasure to meet you!"

Jessica reached out and touched Vulture's head very gently and said, "Likewise."

Vulture blushed. Jessica and Vulture took a liking to each other instantly.

Vulture said, "Oh, Jessica, you are a beautiful woman!"

Jessica said, "Vulture, show me your wings."

Vulture stretched his wings, they were magnificent!

Milo got in the trailer, and Raven closed the door. Jessica got in the pickup and away they went. Vulture disappeared into the sky.

Jessica turned the radio on. The music was great! The Arch Fairies sang along. Happiness radiated from the old pickup. They had covered 350 miles. It was time for another stop. When the pickup stopped, everyone jumped out.

Milo spoke, "It sure is boring riding in that trailer!"

Jessica said, "You should run along with us instead of riding."

Milo said, "Good idea!"

## CHAPTER 19 | **STAR GIRL ASHLEE**

Just then, Milo noticed a young girl walking towards them. Milo sensed there was something strange about the girl, no one else did.

The girl wore a western-style shirt. It was black. It had small silver stars on it. She wore a big, western-style buckle. On her belt, there were words on it. Milo couldn't make the words out.

The girl walked up and slapped Milo on the butt. Milo jumped. He wasn't expecting that!

The girl spoke, "Buckskin Paint! Never did care for Buckskin Paints."

Jessica said, "I really don't care if you like him or not, because he is MY Milo Boy."

Milo spoke, "What are you, some kind of a smart aleck?" And he gave the girl a push with his nose. He was able to read what was written on the buckle— RIDING CHAMPION OF THE STAR DIMENSION.

Milo thought, *Star Dimension…I have heard about that dimension. Didn't know there were horses there.* Milo also looked right into the girl's eyes. They had a star-like twinkle in them.

The girl stepped back. Milo stuck his tongue out at her. The girl began to laugh, and Milo laughed, and Jessica laughed too.

The girl said, "I would like to ride you, Milo."

Milo said, "Get the saddle, Jessica."

The girl said, "I won't need a saddle to ride this old plug."

Milo got a sneer on his face.

The girl snapped her fingers and a riding helmet appeared in her hands. She put the helmet on and tightened the chinstrap.

*Smart girl!*

The helmet had a beautiful star painted on it, it sparkled in the sunlight.

The girl jumped on Milo's back. Milo walked along slowly; the girl kicked him in the ribs. He took off like a shot out of a cannon. The girl shot along Milo's back. Milo put his tail up and stopped her; otherwise she would have gone right off Milo's back. Milo put on his "brakes," and the girl shot forward. Milo put his head up and stopped her.

Milo spoke, "How's that, sweetie?"

Milo sidestepped so quickly—he left her sitting in mid-air and then sidestepped under her and caught her. Then Milo uttered those famous words, "You ain't seen nothing yet!"

Milo put his head down and went into a gallop. And then Milo opened up, it was like riding a Harley at 100 miles per hour with no windshield.

The girl was splattered with bugs. She hollered out, "Please stop, Milo!"

Milo spoke, "Oh no, sweetie!" and Milo bucked. The girl shot eight feet into the air. Milo caught her as she came down. Milo spoke, "How's that for an 'old plug'?"

The girl started to cry, "I am so sorry, Milo." She jumped off Milo. She looked like she had been caught in a tornado.

Milo put his nose on her, and a feeling of brotherhood swept over her. Milo thought that girl was a real know-it-all. *I hope I taught her a lesson! Be careful of how you act and what you say, it could come back and bite you.* Milo chuckled.

Milo told the girl, "You better go and clean up."

The girl said, "Milo, please don't leave. I have to talk to you."

Milo said, "We will wait."

The girl came back, she looked beautiful.  She didn't take long.

"That sure didn't take long." Milo said, "What is your name?"

The girl spoke, "Ashlee is my name. I am from the Star Dimension. The elders of the Star Dimension sent me to see what the world is like. Milo, can I travel with you?"

Milo said, "Ashlee, you can be part of our team."

Ashlee reached up and held Milo's cheeks in each hand, "Oh, thank you, Milo!" She turned and gave Jessica a hug. "Oh, thank you, Jessica!"

They jumped into the pickup and off they went.

"The competition starts tomorrow. Are you ready, Milo?"

"Bring it on," Milo said.

Jessica was up early. She checked her saddle and bridle out. She cleaned her helmet and gave it a polishing. It was a beautiful dark green (Jessica always wore a helmet when she rode). *The Top Being gave me this wonderful mind, I must protect it.*

The competitions began—games like barrels and pole-weaving; the western pleasure class, dressage, and rodeo events. Jessica and Milo won them all. Jessica was so proud of Milo. He was the BEST of the BEST!

Jessica, Milo, and the team loaded up and pulled out. One down and twenty to go. The team pulled into the next fairgrounds. The horse arena was full of horses and trailers and trucks. The old pickup was the oldest rig there. Jessica jumped out and opened the trailer and out stepped Milo. The fairies had groomed Milo—he looked great!

Some of the competitors walked over to look at Milo. They talked amongst themselves. One woman spoke up and said, "What's your horse's name?"

Jessica said, "Milo is my horse's name."

"So this is the horse that was clocked at 80 miles per hour at the derby?" and everyone laughed.

Milo thought, *What a smarty-pants "Miss Pretty-Pretty" is!* He raised his head and sneezed and blew horse snot on her.

Jessica laughed, and the woman stomped away. The rest of the crowd stood around and talked amongst themselves.

Jessica said, "You can stand around and look at Milo all you want, but you will be crying in your beer tonight when Milo gets done with you!"

The people walked away, they were all quiet.

Milo let out a huge whinny, it echoed through the fairgrounds.

Jessica got on Milo. They walked around the fairgrounds.

Milo thought, *Holy Cow, thank you for sending Jessica to me. She is the BEST of the BEST!*

As they walked, a group of young boys (or what Inferno would say, 'a group of young tykes that were green behind the ears yet') walked toward Jessica and Milo.

Jessica gave the boys that smile that lights the sky.

One of the lads tripped over himself, he was so infatuated with Jessica. The lad said, "Nice horse." *He is not even looking at me!*

The lad began to flirt with Jessica. Jessica strung him along.

Milo thought, *That lad really thinks he's cool.* Milo thought some more. *Well, it's time to end this conversation.*

Milo conjured up his mystical powers. He swung his head very slowly towards the lad. Milo's nose touched the lad. The lad reached up and touched Milo's nose, and instantly wet his pants! The lad ran off in shame. Ah, this is the BEST of the BEST!

An old cowboy came walking along. He walked over to Jessica, "Nice horse you got there."

Jessica said, "Thanks."

The old cowboy said, "I've had a horse since I was young."

Jessica said, "His name is Milo."

Milo put his nose on the old cowboy. Milo thought, *The old cowboy smells like a horse…and he smells like tobacco...and he smells like hay and oats. This human is a real person. There is nothing phony about him.*

The old cowboy said, "Jessica, I heard Milo is a fast running horse. I heard he was clocked at eighty miles per hour at the Kentucky Derby. I also heard that he jumped the starting gate. This almost sounds unreal. If I wouldn't have seen the pictures of Milo doing this, I wouldn't have believed it!"

Jessica said, "Yes, it is really hard to comprehend. I really don't like to talk about Milo's achievements. If I did, most people would think I was nuts. All I can say is, Milo is a very special horse—a horse beyond belief, a horse that has mystical powers, a horse that can run as fast as the wind can blow, a horse that has a heart of gold and a soul of fire, a horse that possesses the virtues. Old Cowboy, Milo is the BEST of the BEST!"

The old cowboy said, "Jessica, I do believe. I do believe! I can tell by looking at Milo that Milo is the BEST of the BEST!"

Milo thought, *I must be humble. I must not let Jessica's statements about me go to my head.*

(Remember when Milo ran 300 miles an hour across the desert floor? Even the Holy Cow was amazed at what Milo had done.)

Milo bedded down. It had been a long day. The *Blanket of Sparkling Mist* floated above him, and he slept.

Milo got up early. He walked around and introduced himself to all the horses. Milo touched all of them, and they became brothers. (Horses are magical, mystical animals. Deep down inside, they all love each other.)

Milo wondered if he had proven a point yet. It hurt him to win over them—for these horses were truly the BEST of the BEST!

Milo bowed his head, "Holy Cow, I have broken all the records. Maybe I should quit."

The Holy Cow said, "No not yet. I will tell you when it will end."

## CHAPTER 20 | **PONY AND FROG**

Ashlee, the girl from the Star Dimension, walked through the horses. She noticed a Welsh Pony grazing across the fence. Ashlee took a short run and jumped the six-foot fence with ease (Star Dimension Beings were noted for their jumping abilities).

She walked up to the pony. She said, "Can you talk?"

Pony said, "Yes."

"That's great!" Ashlee said. "What are you doing here?"

Pony said, "I am a loner."

Ashlee said, "Been on your own all your life?"

"Yep," Pony said. "When my brother and I were born, I was in a coma. Ma thought I was dead, so she left me. A mare and her colt picked me up and shook me. I came to. She hollered, 'Walk! Walk or you will die!' I began to walk, I didn't want to die. She let me drink her milk and I became strong. She took care of me for quite a while. Then a rancher came and hauled her and the colt away. I have been on my own ever since."

Ashlee took Pony and led him to Milo. Ashlee told Milo about Pony.

Milo looked at Pony, "You look just like Minute Man, the pony!"

Milo smelled Pony. He said, "You smell just like Minute Man! We call him Pony too. We will take you to Minnesota."

It was time for the competition to begin... Jessica got on Milo and rode him into the staging area. Everyone was quiet. They all had one thing on their minds—winning.

Milo stood in silence. He was very humble.

Jessica scratched him. It made Milo relax.

The competition began, and Milo won each event. When the competition was over, Milo walked back to the trailer. Jessica collected the trophies.

Milo was glad it was over. Milo stood by himself.

Vulture flew in.

"Where you been, Vulture?"

"I was cleaning up road kills."

Milo said, "Good for you, Vulture." And they both laughed.

Raven was out doing some high flying. Milo looked down the road and here came a big leopard frog.

He hopped up to Milo and said, "Hi, Milo, Milo, Milo."

Milo said, "How do you know my name?

"Turtle, Turtle, Turtle told me about you. Besides, all I have heard around here is Milo wins, Milo wins, and Milo wins; so I thought I better come and meet you."

Milo said, "How do you know about Turtle?"

"We communicate you know. Turtle has the same gift Chassie has."

Milo thought aloud, "Ah, Frog, do you know the story about 'The Tortoise and the Hare?'

Frog said, "Yes, I do, but Turtle, Turtle, Turtle made me promise not to tell you."

Milo said, "That Turtle is something! She is always one step ahead of me!"

Raven, Milo, Vulture, and Frog laughed.

Frog said, "Have you got any water, water, water?"

Milo said, "Jump into the pail."

Frog jumped into the water. It felt great! Frog cleaned up and then he jumped into the other pail and drank.

Milo said, "Smart Frog."

Milo dumped the pail that Frog washed up in. He set the pail down, and it filled up again.

Frog drank the water and said, "This is the BEST of the BEST!"

"Yes," Milo said, "it is the water from Mirror Lake."

Frog jumped on Milo's back. It startled Milo, and he jumped sideways.

Frog said, "Sorry, sorry, sorry about that. I have never been this high off the ground, ground, ground. Milo, it is a privilege to sit on you—the kindest, fastest horse from the Special Place, the horse that spreads brotherhood wherever he walks. Someday you will be written about and you will be called 'Milo the Legend, Legend, Legend.'"

Frog jumped up between Milo's ears and sat there. Milo said, "Scratch right there. I am itchy."

And Frog laughed.

Jessica walked up. "Hey, Milo, what's that frog doing between your ears?"

Milo said, "He is my new brother, brother, brother."

Milo said, "Jessica, meet Frog, Frog, Frog."

Milo, Jessica, Raven, Vulture, and Frog all laughed. Frog jumped off Milo and lit on Jessica's shoulder. He kissed her ear, "You are a very beautiful, beautiful, beautiful girl."

Jessica said, "Thank you. Thank you. Thank you." And everyone laughed again.

Frog said, "I am looking for a lake, lake, lake. The old pond dried up."

Jessica said, "We will be going by a lake. We will drop you off."

All the time Vulture sat on top of the trailer, he was eyeing up Frog. *Boy, do I like frogs,* he thought. *Especially after they have been "pancaked" by the human's automobile going nowhere fast.At least automobiles are good for something.*

Frog looked at Vulture. He said, "Hi, Vulture, Vulture, Vulture. Hey, Vulture, what are you thinking about?"

Vulture spoke, "Oh nothing, nothing, nothing." Vulture and Frog laughed.

Frog said, "I bet you are thinking about eating me."

Vulture said, "Well, Frog, I can never tell a lie. You frogs are the BEST of the BEST of the BEST!"

Frog had a wonderful sense of humor. Frog said, "Vulture, Vulture, Vulture, I commend you for never telling a lie, lie, lie. Truth, truth, truth is the BEST of the BEST of the BEST!" And they all laughed, laughed, laughed, and happiness radiated from them.

They were brothers,	brothers,	brothers!

## CHAPTER 21 | **THE OLD COWBOY**

Jessica said, "Let's go talk to the cowboy."

The old cowboy was sitting under a huge oak tree, his horse by his side.

Jessica said, "I want to interview you. I want to know about your life."

The old cowboy laughed, "No one has ever wanted to know about my life!" The old cowboy said, "I will tell you about my whole life…

"Grew up in a small town, lived on a farm, rode horses since I was able to get on one. Worked cattle, roped, did it all. When I went to school, I got good grades—3.8 average. The teachers were great people—they were told what to teach me. I could tell they wanted to try different things—they weren't allowed to. Slowly, they built a box around my head. Television. News. Government. Politicians know best. Churches know best. In my mind, I always questioned everything they told me. Graduated from high school. After graduation ceremony was over, when I walked out the door, I took the box that they built around my head and threw it in the garbage."

Jessica and Milo laughed.

The old cowboy said, "My life has been mainly about horses. I know why you horses do what you do. I know how you think and I know why you are quiet and, Milo, I know you can talk. I can tell by the expression on your face. So, Milo, why don't you talk to me?"

Milo said, "Okay," and laughed. Milo said, "Cowboy, you know how television and movies portray cowboys as drunks, killers, woman chasers, and fighters? Were you ever like that?"

"No, Milo, I was never like that. I never drank alcohol, I was always 'high' on the environment around me—good water, good air, beautiful farmlands, wild animals, domestic animals, riding hard, roping, branding, cutting cattle, medical care of animals. That is what real cowboys are about! Television and movies are all full of it!"

Milo and Jessica laughed.

The cowboy said, "Mountains. I love mountains. I have got a cabin in the foothills, I visit it quite often. I wrote a poem the last time I was there. Want to hear it?"

Milo and Jessica said, "Yes!"

Cowboy said, "I call it 'My Angel Poem.' This is a true poem. This really happened to me."

So the cowboy recited the poem…

IT IS SNOWING IN THE MOUNTAINS.
IT IS CHANGING THEM FROM BROWN TO WHITE
THE SNOW WILL BE IN THE FOOTHILLS BY TONIGHT.
THE SNOW SO WHITE IN COLOR IS COMING MY WAY WHEN I WAKE IN THE MORNING
IT WILL BE A BEAUTIFUL DAY.
WHEN I STEP FROM MY CABIN, THE SNOWFLAKES
WILL BE FLOATING DOWN, ALL DIFFERENT SIZES AND SHAPES.
THEY WILL CHANGE EVERYTHING IN SIGHT FROM BROWN TO WHITE.
THE SNOWFLAKES WILL BE FLOATING FROM A SPECIAL PLACE.
THEY ARE BAPTIZING ME AS THEY TOUCH MY FACE.
I GET A SPECIAL FEELING AS I AM STANDING THERE.
LIKE SOMEONE IS WATCHING ME—SOMEONE THAT REALLY CARES.
I RAISE MY HANDS TO THE SKY AND SAY, THANK YOU FOR THIS SPECIAL DAY!
A FEELING OF SERENITY OVERTAKES MY MIND AND SOUL.
IT TAKES ALL MY THOUGHTS AWAY.

I CAN'T BELIEVE WHAT'S HAPPENING TO ME
ON THIS, MY SPECIAL DAY!
I BOW MY HEAD IN REVERENCE
AND A THOUGHT COMES TO MY MIND,
COULD IT BE MY GUARDIAN ANGEL
THAT IS WATCHING OVER ME?

I WILL MAKE AN ANGEL LIKE I DID SO MANY YEARS AGO.
I WILL MAKE AN ANGEL IN THIS BLESSED SNOW.
AS I LAY IN THE SNOW, IT BEGINS TO COVER ME.
THEN I MAKE THAT ANGEL THAT HAS BEEN WATCHING OVER ME.
I RISE TO MY FEET AND TURN AROUND,
THERE MY BLESSED ANGEL LIES ON THE GROUND.
THE ANGEL BEGINS TO GLOW AND RISES FROM THE SNOW,
AND THEN FOR SURE I KNOW, THIS IS A BLESSED SNOW!
THE ANGEL RISES UP INTO THE SNOW-FILLED SKY AND NOW I KNOW FOR SURE
IT WILL WATCH OVER ME UNTIL THE DAY I DIE.


When Cowboy finished his poem, a tear formed in his eye. His horse brushed it away. "Milo, this horse takes care of me. Milo, I must tell you something else, but I will only tell this story to you."

So Milo and Cowboy walked away from Jessica, and Cowboy told Milo his story.

"Milo, I pitched camp for the night. I started a campfire; I sat down, and took a break. I dozed off. When I awoke, my Paint Horse was gone, and this horse I have got now stood in its place. My saddle and saddle pad and bridle lay on the ground. I was dumbfounded, there were no tracks! It was as if someone had picked the Paint up and put this horse in its tracks. I put the saddle blanket on this horse. It fit perfectly. So did the saddle, so did the bridle. I slapped myself. I was awake, I was alive."

"Milo, I have something else to tell you," he whispered in Milo's ear. "This horse never has gotten old. He has been exactly the same for twenty-five years. This horse knows everything; I did not have to teach him anything."

Milo said, "Cowboy, I know some horses just like that. Some horses will live forever." Milo said, "Your horse came from the Special Place. Your old Paint went to the Special Place. She drank the milk from the Holy Cow and became young again and, now, she will live forever."

The cowboy's horse shook his head up and down.

Milo said, "Cowboy, what is your horse's name?"

"Milo, I named him Silent. He hardly ever makes a sound."

Silent gave Milo a push with his nose and shook his head up and down; he had a huge grin on his face.

Milo said, "Silent, you are the BEST of the BEST of the BEST!"

Jessica walked over to Cowboy, Silent, and Milo. "Milo, we must move out."

They said their goodbyes. Cowboy jumped on Silent and rode off.

Milo said, "There is a human that fits into the world. He is the BEST of the BEST of the BEST!"

Milo and Jessica walked back to the trailer. Ashlee was there with Pony. Vulture sat on top of the trailer. Frog, Frog, Frog floated in the water pail, Raven was picking sand for his gizzard, and the fairies were asleep in the pickup.

Jessica said, "We must leave."

They loaded up and off they went. The fairies hollered out, "Minnesota, here we come!"

They dropped Frog, Frog, Frog at the lake and drove to Minnesota.

They made it to Minnesota that evening. They were tired.

Milo said, "We will sleep here." The *Blanket of Sparkling Mist* hovered over them and they slept.

## CHAPTER 22 | **PONY'S STORY**

Morning broke. Everyone was wide awake. Today, Pony and Minute Man would meet. Would they truly be brothers?

Ashlee led Pony to the fence, she touched the fence, and the wires parted. They stepped into the pasture. Mhilo, Breaker, and Minute Man stood across the pasture.

Minute Man noticed Ashlee and Pony; he took off running towards them. (Minute Man was a feisty pony; he was always ready to agitate. Remember how he called Milo a chicken, chicken, chicken?) Minute Man ran full speed towards Ashlee and Pony, his neck stretched out. He was on a mission.

*Strange pony in my pasture? No way!*

Minute Man ran up to Pony and stopped. "That pony looks just like me!" Minute Man smelled Pony. "That pony smells just like me!"

Pony smelled Minute Man. *Minute Man smells just like me…Minute Man…is…my brother!*

Pony and Minute Man put their heads together, forehead to forehead, and tears rolled down their cheeks. The tears formed in a puddle, they sparkled like diamonds. They could not stop crying.

Ashlee stood with a beautiful smile on her face. A star swooped down from the sky; it picked Ashlee up, and flew away. Her job was completed—Pony and Minute Man were reunited!

The Top Being watched from above and tears formed in His eyes, and the tears formed into a soft rain. And the rain fell on Minute Man and Pony and blessed them. A huge rainbow formed in the sky, and the Top Being walked off across the Universe. Pony and Minute Man would live forever.

Milo looked at Jessica, Raven, Vulture, and the fairies. Milo said, "I was going to go to Canada but I'm exhausted. I must go on vacation!"

Jessica said her goodbyes to Milo, Raven, Vulture, and the fairies. She got in the old pickup and drove away. As she drove away Milo hollered out. "How's the glove box?" Jessica gave Milo the thumbs up!

Frog would say, "What a woman, woman, woman—a beautiful, wonderful woman, woman, woman." A woman that fits into the world. The world will be a better place because of Jessica. This is the BEST of the BEST of the BEST! (Oh, by the way, the glove box in the old pickup will always be full of money!)

Milo, Vulture, the fairies, and Raven went looking for a portal. Everyone needed a vacation. Milo was tired; the competition was really not his "cup of tea." He couldn't wait to get to Mirror Lake and do some goofing off!

The gang walked along slowly, sniffing for that wonderful, fresh air that came from their dimension. It took half a day and, finally, the Arch Fairies found the portal.

They put the *Blanket of Sparkling Mist* over the portal. Milo stuck his head through and checked it out. "Yep, this is it!" and he stepped into his dimension. (Milo always checked first before he walked in. Remember when he almost stepped into the abyss? After that, he vowed to always look before he jumped.)

Milo sucked in that beautiful air that was in the dimension that he was born in. It felt good in his lungs. It wouldn't be long before he would be at Mirror Lake. Milo broke over the big hill and there it was— sparkling as ever!

*Trees! Look at the trees!* Trees dotted the landscape around the lake. (The Holy Cow had planted trees while Milo was gone.) There were all kinds of different trees.

Raven hollered out, "This is the BEST of the BEST!"

There was a huge, dead tree that towered above the rest. It was a perfect "Vulture Roost." Vulture flew to the highest limb and lit. *It just don't get any better that this!* He could see for miles.

Milo walked to the lake. There was a big tree, it had apples on it. Yes, it was an apple tree—with all different kinds of apples hanging on it!

The fairies flew into the tree. They picked an apple and tasted it. They loved it! The Arch Fairies picked an apple and brought it to Milo. Milo took a small bite. Milo couldn't believe how wonderful it tasted! Milo ate the whole apple. It was the BEST of the BEST of the BEST!"

Milo thought, *Trees…Apples…Water…This is truly the gift of life.* It didn't get any better than this. *Thank you! Thank you! Thank you!* Milo laughed. Frog had definitely made an impression on Milo.

Milo lay down. He thought he had better rest up.

The fairies laid the *Blanket of Sparkling Mist* over him. They tucked in the edges. They petted Milo's nose and began to hum, and Milo fell into a deep sleep.

Milo had a dream. He dreamed about all the horses he met, every single one. Their minds were clear and clean: the feisty ones, the dominant ones, the champions, and the quiet ones. They all had one thing in common. They were all brothers, brothers, brothers, they were all proud to be horses…AND they were all glad they had four legs!

Milo chuckled in his sleep. "We are the BEST of the BEST of the BEST! If only humans were like us horses, there would be peace in the entire world."

Milo's dream drifted away.

## CHAPTER 23 | **MILO MEETS THE PRAIRIE DOGS**

Milo awoke. The fairies were in the apple tree. They loved apples! Milo walked over to the apple tree. The Arch Fairies threw Milo two apples. Milo ate both of them. Milo told the fairies he was going to go for a walk.

The fairies said, "We will stay here."

Milo trotted off. Up the hill he went. Milo's trot was beautiful. He covered about ten miles and came to an abrupt halt. The ground ahead was covered with dirt mounds and holes. They were prairie dog holes.

A prairie dog popped out of a hole. She spoke, "Hi, horse, how are you today?"

Milo said, "Hi, prairie dog, looks like you have been busy."

And then prairie dogs popped out of all the holes. Milo laughed, and the prairie dogs all laughed together. They were a happy bunch.

"Where are you headed, horse?"

Milo said, "Oh, just trotting around."

The prairie dog said, "Well, if you want to keep going, I will show you how to get through this 'minefield' that we have got here." And everyone laughed.

Milo said, "Okay."

So the prairie dog led Milo through the "minefield." The prairie dog said, "Horse, we have seen another horse out here."

Milo said, "Really?"

"Yes," the prairie dog said. "He is a real beauty!"

Milo said, "I am going to see if I can find him." And Milo trotted off.

Milo broke over a hill, and ahead was a beautiful field of red clover. It smelled great! Milo walked along, tasting the red clover buds. They were sweet (Milo kind of liked sweet-tasting food).

Milo looked ahead, and there stood a horse on the far side of the field. Milo walked toward the horse, and the horse walked toward Milo. They met in the middle of the field.

They both spoke at the same time, "Hi, horse!" And they both laughed.

Milo thought, *What a beautiful horse! He must be a Thoroughbred!* He was taller than the horses he had competed against. *And he is taller than me!* Milo thought, *he is even bigger than Bravo!*

Milo said, "Where you from?"

The horse said, "I am from the Special Place, but I come here quite often."

Milo said, "I have never been to the Special Place. Hey, do you know the Holy Cow?"

"Yes, I do, horse. You see, horse, I came from the world. I was a racehorse. I got old and went to the Special Place and became young again. And now I will live forever."

Milo and the horse laughed. The Thoroughbred said, "Hey, horse, I want to tell you something I have never told anyone else."

Milo said, "What's that?"

The Thoroughbred said, "You have to keep this a secret, you know. When I come here, there is a Human that comes here and rides me. He seems to have great powers and he descends from above. He dresses in a long white robe trimmed in gold. He wears a purple sash. Sometimes he speaks in parables, and I don't understand what he means. We have a lot of fun. He laughs, and I laugh, and I give him the ride of a lifetime. When we are finished, he disappears, and I travel back to the Special Place."

Milo said, "Well I have to leave. It is great to meet you! Oh, by the way, what is your name?"

The big Thoroughbred reared up, "Secretariat is my name. What's yours?"

Milo reared up, "Milo is my name." And they parted company.

Milo headed back to Mirror Lake. He got to the prairie dog "minefield." The head prairie dog led him

through the "minefield." All the prairie dogs popped out of their holes and hollered, "Hip-Hip-Hooray!" And Milo trotted away.

Milo reached Mirror Lake. The fairies were skipping across the water. Raven was flying high.

Vulture flew off his roost and lit in front of Milo. He spoke, "Milo, where you been?"

Milo said, "I did some trotting around, ran into a prairie dog 'minefield,' talked to some prairie dogs, and traveled on. Ran into a big Thoroughbred horse, we talked. He was from the Special Place."

Vulture said, "What was the Thoroughbred's name?"

Milo said, "The horse's name was Secretariat."

Vulture hopped into the air, "Holy Cow, Milo! He is the most famous horse to ever walk on the face of the earth!"

Milo said, "Earth?"

"Yes, Milo, that is another name for the world."

Milo said, "Secretariat was a very humble horse. He never said a word about how great he is—he was so kind. I really enjoyed meeting him."

"Milo, did you tell him about YOUR running ability?"

Milo said, "No."

Vulture said, "Milo, you and Secretariat are humble horses. Humility is the BEST of the BEST of the BEST." Vulture spread his beautiful wings and flew to his roost.

Milo was tired. He lay down under the apple tree. He pulled the *Blanket of Sparkling Mist* over himself. He thought about the prairie dogs—they were so happy. He said, "I must bring the fairies to meet them. And then there was Secretariat, what a wonderful horse! I hope to see him again."

Milo yawned and went to sleep.

## CHAPTER 24 | **THE RIDE OF A LIFETIME**

It was time to wake. Milo looked up at the apple tree. An apple fell from the tree. Milo caught it in his mouth. He bit it in two and ate it. The apple tasted so good!

*Apples, apples, apples. They are the BEST of the BEST of the BEST!*  Milo laughed, he jumped to his feet, and hollered out, "Wake up, fairies, we are going to see the prairie dogs."

The fairies had been asleep in the apple tree. They jumped from the tree and lit on Milo's back.

Raven and Vulture flew in, "Where are you headed, Milo?"

"We are going to go and visit the prairie dogs. Come with us."

So off they went. Milo trotted along at a brisk pace. Soon they were at the prairie dog "minefield".

Milo stomped the ground and all the prairie dogs popped out of their holes. "Hi, Milo!" they hollered out and they all began to laugh. What a happy bunch they were!

The head prairie dog said, "Milo, come with us."

They raced to the top of a big hill. "Hey, Milo, watch this!" And they all did somersaults together down the hill.

*I wonder if I can do that? No, I better just roll down the hill.* So Milo rolled. It was a blast! Milo played with the prairie dogs for a while. It was such fun!

Milo said, "Well, prairie dogs, I must leave." And they parted company.

Raven and Vulture flew above. They really liked the prairie dogs. The fairies couldn't believe how agile they were. The fairies said, "Milo, that is the first time we have seen prairie dogs. They are fantastic, and they are all so happy! And, Milo, they all have four legs!"

Milo laughed and said, "Let's move on. Maybe we will run into Secretariat."

They reached the clover field where Milo had seen Secretariat. He was nowhere in sight. Milo walked to the middle of the field and stopped. He sensed that there was a human watching him. His eyes scanned the horizon. No one was in sight.

Raven and Vulture flew in, "Hey, Milo, there is a human just over that small rise. It is a girl human. She is walking towards you."

And then Milo spotted her. Milo stood perfectly still, and the girl walked up to Milo.

The girl was beautiful. She spoke, "Hello, Milo."

"Boy," Milo said, "how do you know my name?"

The girl spoke, "Oh, Milo, Chassie told me all about you."

Milo said, "I didn't know that there were humans that lived in the Special Place."

"Humans do not live in the Special Place, Milo. We are only allowed to visit the Special Place. You see, Milo, only the humans that love horses are allowed to visit. I was allowed to pass from the Special Place for humans to your dimension because I wanted to ride you."

Milo laughed, "Jessica, Ashlee, and now you. By the way, what's your name?"

The girl spoke, "My name is Carla. I have come from the world, and now I live in peace—in a Special Place where humans go when they leave the world. Milo, when Chassie told me that you can run faster than the wind, I instantly wanted to ride you. The Top Being gave me permission."

Milo said, "Jump on, Carla, and I will give you the ride of a lifetime!"

So Carla jumped on Milo's back. The fairies flew out of Milo's mane. Carla was awestruck, "What are they, Milo?"

"They are fairies, Carla. They are guardians."

Carla said, "How do they fly? They have no wings."

"Carla, they fly on magnetic fields. That is why they glow."

Carla said, "They are different colors."

"Yes, Carla, and they can change colors."

Raven flew in and lit on the ground. "Hi, Carla, how are you?"

Carla laughed, "A raven that talks!"

"Oh, yes, Carla."

Carla looked up at Vulture circling overhead, "Hi, Carla, welcome to Milo's world."

Carla laughed. She thought, *This is amazing!* "Hey Milo, how fast can you run?"

"I can run 300 miles per hour, Carla. When I get to 100 miles per hour, a magnetic field forms around me and this is how I accomplish this kind of speed. I will only run at seventy miles per hour when you ride me."

Carla said, "Oh, Milo that is plenty fast enough for me." And Milo and Carla laughed.

Milo began to walk, his walk was quite fast, and then he did all the different gaits that horses do. Carla was impressed with Milo's skill. He never missed a single one.

Milo stopped, "What do you think of that, Carla?"

"You are one of a kind, Milo, one of a kind."

Milo said, "It is time for me to show you what it is like to ride a horse at seventy, so hang on."

Carla couldn't believe how smooth Milo's gallop was. Milo was headed for a blown down tree. He would have to jump twelve feet high to clear it. Carla held on, and Milo made the jump and came to a stop.

"Get off me, Carla. I want to show you what else I can do." So Milo did the Lipizzaner hop, and then he did some dance steps.

Carla laughed and clapped her hands.

"Well," Milo said, "that is all I've got."

Carla said her goodbyes to everyone, and she slowly walked away shaking her head. It was unbelievable what that Milo Boy could do. He was truly the BEST of the BEST of the BEST!

Milo headed back to Mirror Lake. When he got to the prairie dog "minefield," he stomped his foot, and the prairie dogs popped out of their holes. They ran to Milo and encircled him and they sang a little prairie dog song for Milo.

Milo loved their song. It was a very happy song. Milo said his goodbyes and moved on.

When Milo and the team got back to Mirror Lake, they were all exhausted. They pulled the *Blanket of Sparkling Mist* over Milo and themselves and went to sleep.

Milo lay awake. He thought about what he had done. He had showed Carla all the different gaits of horses, many of them not natural to a horse. Milo thought about how many of the unnatural gaits were brought about by training and breeding. Humans seemed to never be satisfied with the natural ability of a horse. They demand so much from a horse and so little from themselves. They are such a feeble species. Their walk is slow, their run is slow, their reflexes are slow, their jumps are feeble, and their minds are strange.

*I am so glad I am a horse! Thank you, Top Being and Holy Cow, for giving me four legs. For all us horses are truly the BEST of the BEST of the BEST!*

Milo stretched, he got a beautiful grin on his face, and then he spoke, "As Frog would say, 'Life, life, life is good, good, good.'" And he chuckled and went to sleep.

The moon and the stars sparkled in the sky. The Top Being looked down on Milo and he spoke, "As Frog would say, 'bless you, bless you, bless you, Milo.'" And He smiled and walked off across the Universe.

## CHAPTER 25 | **THE WHITE-TAILED DEER**

When Milo awoke, a feeling of peace and serenity filled his body. *Why do I feel so good?* (What he didn't know was how, that night, the Top Being had given him a special blessing that would strengthen him, physically and spiritually.)

Milo stood. He looked across Mirror Lake. It was beautiful.

Vulture flew down from his roost. He lit in front of Milo. "Boy, Milo, you sure do have beautiful eyeballs." Milo and Vulture began to laugh. Milo spun around and gave Vulture a gentle kick. Vulture did a double back-flip and lit on his feet and they both laughed, laughed, laughed.

The fairies awoke, "Hey, Milo, we will bet you a buck that you don't know where we are going next."

Milo said, "Boy, I really don't have a clue."

The fairies laughed.

Milo thought the word "buck" seemed to ring a bell in his mind.

The fairies sang, "Heigh-Ho Heigh-Ho, it's off to work we go…" and the gang marched off.

Milo thought, *Same old story. I can tell those fairies are looking for a portal.*

Vulture was flying along. Raven flew in; he was headed right for Vulture. He pulled up and lit on Vulture's back. It was no problem for Vulture—he could carry Raven like nothing. His wings were large and powerful.

Raven started to sing, "Get along, little doggy. Get along, little doggy…"

Vulture did a loop, and Raven slipped off.

Milo said, "How wonderful they are!"

The fairies flew ahead of Milo, each one giving off a different colored light.

They looked like a bunch of bumblebees. Milo thought about the big honeybee and how much he loved the honey that he ate.

While Milo was daydreaming, the fairies had gained quite a distance on Milo. So Milo broke into a pace, he seemed to glide along effortlessly. Soon he caught the fairies, "So fairies, where are we headed?"

"Milo, we are in search of a portal that will let us into the world. It will be a portal into the northern woods of Minnesota. We want you to meet the animal of peace."

Milo said, "And who is the animal of peace?"

"Milo, the animal of peace is the white-tailed deer." The fairies came to an abrupt halt. "Listen, Milo. What do you hear?"

Milo said, "I hear a buzzing sound."

"Yes, Milo, it is the sound of bugs—flying insects that love to bite. There is a portal here, a portal into the forest of northern Minnesota. Milo, you will now understand what your tail is for."

They held the *Blanket of Sparkling Mist* in front of Milo. He stuck his head through the portal. He was looking at a dense forest of trees.

A mosquito lit on his nose and started to drill in. Milo jerked his head out of the hole. The mosquito bite made his nose itch. Milo rubbed his nose on his leg.

The fairies laughed, "Well, Milo, welcome to northern Minnesota."

Milo stepped through the portal.

The insects instantly attacked Milo. Milo switched his tail and began swatting flying insects. The deer flies, mosquitoes, dog flies, horse flies, and "no-see-ums" attacked Milo with a vengeance.

Milo began to stamp his feet, "Hey, fairies, this is nuts!"

The fairies laughed. They encircled Milo and covered him with a light green mist. The insects flew away. The light green mist cooled his itching body. "Thank you, fairies. I don't think I could have taken very much more of that!"

Milo walked through the forest of northern Minnesota. His goal was to meet the majestic white-tailed deer.

The deer that lived on brush, buds, and weed seeds for five months over the winter in Minnesota.

The deer that lived in up to four feet of snow and cold temperatures of zero to forty-five below.

The deer that have to stave off predators—the coyote, the cougar, and the mighty timber wolf.

The northern Minnesota white-tailed deer is the toughest of the toughest of the toughest…as Frog would say.

(Milo loved Frog; he was so happy, happy, happy and he made everyone laugh, laugh, laugh.)

Milo sniffed the air. He could smell the scent of deer poop. *There has to be a deer in the area.* Milo saw a white flash bounding through the trees. It was a whitetail on the run.

Milo stopped and held perfectly still. He could hear the rustle of the brush. Something was walking towards him. Milo got a big grin on his face. For sure, it was a whitetail walking toward him!

The whitetail appeared. It was a majestic buck. He was beautiful!

Milo was impressed by his facial markings. Milo thought, *The Top Being did a wonderful job when he made the whitetail…and he has four legs.*

Milo spoke, "Hi, deer, it is great to see you!"

The buck nodded his head. His antlers were awesome! The deer spoke, "Horse, what are you doing in the forest?"

Milo said, "I came here to meet you, the white-tailed deer. I have heard many stories about you. You are the animal of peace. You prey on no one. You are truly one of the animals of peace."

Buck spoke, "Yes, Milo, we are peaceful and we all live in peace and we all run together because we are brothers. The Top Being put deer on earth to give humans a wonderful meat. A meat full of protein food that is good for them; a food that humans do not have to consume every day, but a food that will keep them alive.

"Many humans do not understand what we are really about. They do not have any feelings for a whitetail deer. They love wolves and predators that kill us. The wolves are merciless; they hamstring us and take bites out of our hindquarters, and we slowly die from loss of blood. In other words, they eat us alive.

"Coyotes follow the same death pattern. Humans love the predator's ways because they are predators themselves. Humans do not eat wolf meat. They do not need their meat to live, yet they idolize wolves. Do humans love the way the wolf makes the kill? Could be, humans are a strange species.

"Humans own wolves. They build wolf centers. They brainwash their children into thinking they are sweet, little pets. 'It is,' the old cowboy would say, 'it is part of the box that they built around their heads.'"

Milo spoke, "Yes, Buck, the humans got it all wrong. They should tear down the wolf centers and build a whitetail deer center in its place!"

Buck said, "You got it, Milo!" And they both laughed.

Buck stomped his front foot and white-tailed deer came out of the woods. Does, fawns, small bucks, big bucks surrounded Milo and the big Buck…and they began to sing. It was a song of peace and a song of brotherhood. And the big Buck touched Milo with his nose, and a feeling of peace swept over Milo.

Milo bowed his head and then he spoke, "Deer, I will spread the word in my travels. I will tell everyone what you are about, and someday the wolf center will come down!" Milo turned and walked away.

The deer gave Milo the "Hip-Hip-Hooray!" salute.

Milo walked out of the dense forest. He came to a logging road. He walked along the road and came to a small cabin. There was a human and a dog sitting on the cabin porch.

The human looked up. He was surprised to see a horse walking his way. The dog did not bark; he wagged his tail in friendship. The human spoke, "Hi horse, how are you today?"

Milo spoke, "I am just fine."

The human was startled when Milo spoke. He stood up and walked over to Milo. He touched Milo on the withers and scratched him.

Milo said, "Wow, does that feel good!"

The human laughed.

Milo said, "What is your name?"

"My name is Aaron, horse. What is your name?"

"Milo is my name."

The dog came over to Milo and Aaron. The dog was a huge Irish Wolfhound. Milo thought he was such a majestic specimen, so big but so elegant-looking.

The top of the dog's back was thirty-six inches above the ground, his colors were beautiful. Milo could tell the dog was built for running.

The dog's jaws were big and almost scary-looking, but the dog's eyes had a kind look in them.

He sat down and said, "What a beautiful Paint Horse you are."

Aaron looked at his dog. He said, "I didn't know you could talk!"

"Well Aaron, I can talk. I was always afraid that if you knew I could talk you would make a spectacle of me."

Aaron bent down and hugged his dog. "I would never do that to you."

Milo asked, "Dog, what is your name?"

"My name is David. Aaron named me after his father."

Milo said. "That is really different!"

"Yes Milo, Aaron is one of a kind!" And Milo, David and Aaron laughed.

Milo spoke, "Aaron, why do you live in the forest?"

Aaron said, "Milo I could not stand to live around humans anymore. I needed to live in peace and this is the only place I can do this."

"Yes," Milo said, "the forest is a very peaceful place."

David said, "There are only a few predators that you have to be careful around, the wolf, the bear, and the cougar. If you respect them, they will usually leave you alone. I am careful around wolves because they will kill dogs if they get a chance. But all in all, I get along with the predators."

Milo said, "Oh yes David, with your size I bet you do, and David, I commend you for being so understanding."

"Oh yes, Milo, for I have been around since the beginning of time, and the timber wolf knows that if I want to, I can really put the hurt on them!"

The dog stood on his hind legs. He was so tall he could look Milo right in the eyes. "Would you like to race Milo?"

"Oh David, I would love to race you." David knew he could run with horses, but he did not know about Milo's special gift. They walked to a straight stretch in the logging road; it was one quarter mile long. Half of the quarter was downhill, half was uphill. It was a great place to test speed and endurance. The road had some fresh clover growing in it. Milo tested the road. He thought, *feels a little slippery. I better be careful.* David paced back and forth, he limbered up his muscles.

"Are you ready Milo?"

"Yes, I am ready."

A snowshoe rabbit stepped in front of David and Milo. He had come to the road to eat clover and dandelions.

"Hey Rabbit, watch out, we are going to race!"

"Can I race too?"

"Yes, if you want." David and Milo laughed, the rabbit did not laugh. The three of them lined up. Aaron would be the starter. Aaron dropped his arm, and off they went! The rabbit exploded off the starting line, his little legs a blur. He actually was in the lead. He held that position for 300 feet, and then Milo and David pulled alongside. As Milo and David passed him, the rabbit used his last burst of energy and jumped on David's back! David was so excited he did not notice that rabbit had jumped on his back. David and Milo ran neck and neck. Milo was surprised how fast David could run. Every time Milo tried to speed up, his hooves would slip on the fresh clover surface. David's paws really had traction, his toenails dug deep into the ground.

The finish line loomed ahead. The horse and the dog were still neck and neck. When they were two feet from the finish line, the rabbit mustered all his strength. He gave a mighty jump, and crossed the finish line ahead of Milo and David. Milo and David tied in the race. The rabbit jumped for joy. He laughed, and Milo laughed, and David laughed. It was a perfect time in their lives.

You all be the judge.

Did the rabbit really win? He did cross the finish line first. Why did Milo tie? He could have kicked in his magical powers and blew them all away!

He did not do this. He wanted to treat the dog and the rabbit fairly. That is why he ran the race like a regular horse, for being fair to our brothers is a great virtue.

Aaron, David, and Milo returned to the cabin.

The rabbit hopped off into the forest.

Aaron said, "Milo, I have a treat for you." He set a pail of oats in front of Milo. Milo tasted the oats. They were delicious! Milo had never tasted oats. He loved them!

Milo finished eating and said, "I must leave." They said their goodbyes, and Milo trotted off. Milo thought, *I did not have to touch Aaron and David and Rabbit with my nose because brotherhood radiated from them.* And Milo began to sing.

All the time Milo, Aaron, and David were talking, Raven and Vulture and the fairies were flying high in the sky. An eagle was circling with them. The eagle and Vulture and Raven talked about the clean air in northern Minnesota.

The eagle flew them over three majestic lakes in the area. They looked down on Milo. They saw he was moving out, so they said their goodbyes and dove toward Milo.

Raven and Vulture pulled out of their dive and lit in front of Milo.

Milo said, "Where have you guys been?"

"We have been flying with Eagle."

Milo said, "I have never seen an eagle up close."

"Oh, Milo, they are a majestic bird. They look almost sacred."

"You mean you get the same feeling when you look at the eagle that you get when you look at Justice?"

"Yes, Milo, and believe it or not, the eagle chants."

"You have got to be kidding!"

"Oh, no, Milo, the eagle chants just like Justice."

Milo bowed his head, "Sacred, they are. Sacred, they are."

## CHAPTER 26 | **TIMBER WOLVES**

Milo loved the whitetail deer. A feeling of sorrow came over him when he thought about the way they died in the jaws of the timber wolf.

He asked himself, "I wonder why they kill in such an inhumane way. They cut the deer's hamstrings. The deer cannot run; he falls to the ground. They take bites out of their hindquarters. The blood pours from their wounds. The deer bleats from the pain. The deer lives for many hours as they eat them alive.

When the wolf is full, he leaves his prey. But he comes back to eat again. The deer is still alive. The wolf does not kill the deer; he continues to eat the live deer. Hours later, the deer finally dies from trauma and blood loss.

The wolf could have killed the deer with a bite to the deer's neck. His powerful jaws would crush the deer's spinal cord, and the deer would die almost instantly."

Milo spoke to his friends, "Fairies, why are the timber wolves this way?"

"Milo, in the world there are evil things. There are evil humans. Evil roams through the world. It seeks out faith, hope, love, charity, and brotherhood and it destroys it.

"The timber wolf is possessed with evil. When this possession took place, we do not know. But it happened a short time after the wolf was created. Evil is a strange and powerful force. It enters many humans and turns them into wolves, and they kill mercilessly.

"Yes, Milo, you must be very careful. Evil will try to enter your body. It will try to destroy you. It will try to eat you alive.

"We think evil could have been created to test good…to see if you have the willpower to fight it off. We think that this test could very well have been created by the Top Being, but we cannot say for sure. It is one of the great mysteries.

"So, Milo, you must be ready to fight evil—mentally and physically. The white-tailed deer can fight evil mentally but not physically. That's why it is called the animal of peace. When the whitetail dies to nourish evil, it will be called a martyr for peace and it will be given a special reward from the Top Being.

"Like we said before, the whitetail deer was created for its special meat for humans; it is not to be wasted. And the deer was not created for evil, it was created for goodness, and we must respect the deer."

Milo walked through the woods. He thought about everything the fairies had told him. He took everything the fairies had told him seriously. He understood it all. He was not confused AT ALL!

(Remember how sometimes Milo would get confused? Not this time! Milo was dead serious!)

Another challenge was handed to Milo. He would fight evil with all his mind, heart, and soul. Not only that, he would fight evil physically (and we all know with Milo's speed and reflexes that evil would never overtake him).

Milo reared up and whinnied. All the animals, all the birds, all the living things in the world heard the whinny. And Evil heard the whinny and it shrunk back and began to shiver. (The battle has begun!)

Milo walked along the old logging road. It was a beautiful day. All of a sudden, Milo smelled a strange smell he had never smelled before. It made Milo edgy, he became alert. His eyes focused in all directions. He stopped and listened. He could hear rustling in the brush and running steps. They were not real loud. He heard a panting sound, and from behind him came five timber wolves—at breakneck speed!

Milo began to run. He let the wolves slowly gain on him. (He was surprised how fast they could run. Of course, they were no match for Milo's speed.) Milo zeroed in on them, like a horse does before the kick. His eyes narrowed and a sinister look spread across his face.

The wolves closed the distance. When they were in kicking range, Milo let go with his laser-guided kicks. Five kicks scored a direct hit! All five wolves were killed instantly.

Milo spun around. The wolves lay dead; the smell of evil filled the air. Milo walked over to them. Blood covered the ground around them. They all had the look of death on their faces, their teeth were bared. Milo touched each wolf with his nose, and brotherhood entered their dead bodies. The wolves' devastating wounds slowly disappeared. The blood disappeared. They started to stir. They slowly sat up. Milo was amazed at what was happening to each of them. The smell of evil was gone.

Milo spoke, "Wolves go forth and tell your brothers what has happened here today. They will not smell evil on you. They will try to kill you, but you will be protected by the great whitetail's spirit. When the evil wolves teeth touch you, evil will die and good will replace evil and peace will prevail. From this day forward, the timber wolves will kill with a bite to the neck. Never will they hamstring and torture again."

It was Milo's first miracle. The fairies, Vulture, and Raven could not believe what they had witnessed. From that day forward, Milo carried a faint smell of heaven on him. It would never go away.

The fairies flew around Milo. They spoke, "Milo, we must keep on the move."

## CHAPTER 27 | **THE DAMN BEAVERS**

It was getting dark. The moon broke the horizon; it lit up the forest.

Milo could hear a munching sound, and then he heard a splashing sound. "There must be water ahead." Milo walked toward the sound. "Hey, fairies, what is that sound?"

"We will fly ahead and check it out." The fairies flew ahead and soon they were back.

"It's beavers, Milo!"

"Beavers? What are beavers?"

"Well, Milo, follow us," and they all laughed.

Milo saw the glitter of water through the trees and then a huge pond appeared in the moonlight.

Milo could still hear that munching sound, and then a big aspen tree started to fall!

Milo jumped back as the tree fell.

Milo peered through the moonlight and there, at the base of the aspen, were two small animals jumping up and down and laughing. Milo walked toward the beavers.

The beavers noticed Milo. They ran for the pond and jumped in. There was a huge splash as they hit the water. They slapped the water with their paddle tails and dove under. The beavers had never seen a horse and it scared the daylights out of them!

The fairies flew across the pond, their glow reflecting off the water. It was a beautiful sight! They located the two beavers and talked to them. They persuaded them to swim back and talk to Milo.

The beavers swam back and walked up on land. They walked over to Milo.

They spoke, "And what animal species are you?"

"I am a horse and my name is Milo."

"Glad to meet you, horse."

"Glad to meet you, beavers." Milo noticed their teeth. They glistened in the moonlight. "What beautiful teeth you have!"

"The better to cut wood with, Milo."

Milo thought the old vampire, Bugsy, Minute Man's friend, would love to have a set of teeth like theirs. And he laughed inside.

"Hey, Milo, come with us. We want to show you the dam we built."

*Dam? What is a dam?*

They walked to the far end of the pond. "Well, Milo, what do you think of our dam?"

"Damn! That is one big dam!"

"Yes, Milo, we are the best damn dam builders in the world."

"Damn it, you surely are," and everyone laughed.

Milo said, "Fairies, this is the best damn fun I've had in a long time!"

The fairies laughed. The beavers laughed, and they jumped into the pond. They slapped their paddle tails on the water and dove under.

The fairies said, "Let's move out, Milo."

*I wonder why I like to say the word "damn?"* He smiled and started to sing.

## CHAPTER 28 | **BACK AT THE MINNESOTA FARM**

Milo trotted along. The night was beautiful. Milo thought, *The stars are beautiful. I wonder how Ashlee the Star Girl is.*

Milo looked up. A shooting star streaked across the sky, and then a shooting star wrote in the sky: "MILO BOY, YOU BUCKSKIN PAINT, I LOVE YOU! FROM ASHLEE, THE STAR GIRL."

A tear formed in Milo's eye. Milo thought it sure was nice to be loved!

He reared up and let out a huge whinny!

It echoed across the Universe….

The Top Being smiled and said, "Oh, that's my boy, Milo!"

The fairies flew out of Milo's mane. They picked Milo up and flew him over the treetops. They were headed south. Their next stop would be the Minnesota farm.

The fairies set Milo down in a small opening in the trees. "We are not too far from the farm, Milo. We will rest here."

They pulled the *Blanket of Sparkling Mist* over Milo, and they all went to sleep.

Morning came and the sun rose and it warmed the forest.

The fairies awoke. Milo was still sleeping. The fairies said, "We haven't pulled Milo's ears to wake him for a long time." So they pulled Milo's ears.

Milo awoke, "Please don't pull my ears." Milo said, "Hey, fairies, you never have told me about the ear thing."

The fairies said, "We will tell you now. Milo, when the Top Being created horses, mules, and donkeys, he gave them all the same kind of ears. It was hard to tell the difference between them when you first looked at them.

"The Top Being said, 'This will never do.' So instead of devising a new ear for the horse, he just shortened the ears on a horse. This put the nerve endings close to the tips of a horse's ear. That's why they are sensitive.

"It made the horse look much better. It gave the horse a very elegant look. That is why you are so attractive, Milo."

"Well, Milo, we must move out."

They came to a power line. They walked along; they came to a fence line and a gate.

The fairies said, "Milo, we are at the farm." They opened the gate and walked into the pasture. Breaker, Minute Man, Mhilo, Pony, and Summer—the new horse—were grazing.

Mhilo noticed Milo first. He took off at a pace, and Milo paced toward him. The horses seemed to glide across the pasture. It was a sight to behold!

When Mhilo and Milo reached each other, they touched their noses together and spoke at the same time. "My brother," their voices were identical in sound.

The other horses noticed Mhilo and Milo. They came running to them. They were so glad to see each other! Summer stood back.

Breaker said, "Milo, I want you to meet Smart Summer Image! We call her Summer."

Summer stepped up to Milo, "It is a pleasure to meet you, Milo. Everyone has told me about you."

Breaker said, "Milo, come with me." Breaker and Milo walked to the little hill. "Milo, I was really lonesome when Ma went to the Special Place. It was a long, cold winter. Ma talked to me and she kept my spirits up, and then she told me that she—and the Holy Cow—would send a gift to me when spring came.

"One day, the human's pickup pulled into the yard with the horse trailer. They opened the trailer and out stepped Summer! They put Summer in the pasture. She walked over to me and said, 'Breaker, I have come to comfort you and be your friend.' Milo, she is so nice to me. She is a lot like my mother Chassie."

Milo said, "She is very beautiful."

"Yes, Milo, and she is a real runner! She raced in a Quarter Horse race at a fair and won. She is also good at gaming."

Milo said, "I am so happy for you, Breaker!" and they both laughed.

Mhilo came at a pace over to Milo and Breaker; it was as if he was floating in mid-air. "So, Mhilo, what have you been doing?" Milo asked.

Mhilo said, "I have been competing in the games. We are going to the state meet and then to the Champ Show. It is the BEST of the BEST of the BEST!"

Minute Man and Pony walked over to Milo. "Hey, Milo, do you want to fight?"

"No, Minute Man. Remember, I am a chicken, chicken, chicken." And everyone laughed.

Pony spoke up, "Milo, as Frog would say, 'Life here is great, great, great!'" And Pony bucked.

And everyone hollered, "Hip-Hip-Hooray!"

Just then, Raven and Vulture swooped in. They surprised Summer, and she jumped sideways and took off at a fast trot.

Everyone laughed, "Come back, Summer, and meet Raven and Vulture!"

She walked back, and Raven and Vulture introduced themselves.

Summer liked Vulture and Raven. She looked at them very closely. She stretched her neck out and touched them with her nose.

Summer had never paid much attention to birds; she was always too busy eating. (Her muscular body required a lot of good grass, hay, and grains. She was not only physically fit, she was kind and thoughtful. She was easy to catch, and she was loved by all the other horses.)

Minute Man and Pony took Milo aside, "Milo, the old vampire wants to meet you."

"Really? I would love to meet him!"

So Minute Man and Pony told Milo that tonight was the night for the old vampire to come out and do his flying. "Milo, we will meet you tonight at twelve o'clock at the barn."

Vulture and Raven were flying around, and Summer was watching them. They flew in close formation. They showed Summer their flying tricks.

She was amazed! She hollered out, "You birds, be careful so you don't collide!"

"Yes, Summer!" (Motherly instincts showed, even if she was not a mother.)

Milo and the other horses talked about the good old times.

Mhilo talked about his previous owners. He said, "You know, Milo, I was lucky. They treated me well. My problem was my own. I just had a mean streak in me when it came to associating with other horses. That has completely gone away. I thank you for that, Milo."

The fairies said, "It is time to rest." The sun was going down, soon it would be dark. They pulled the *Blanket of Sparkling Mist* over Milo. It was time to sleep.

## CHAPTER 29 | **OLD VAMPIRE HORATIO**

Twelve o'clock—midnight—came. Milo got up. He did not wake the fairies. Milo walked toward the barn. There stood Minute Man, the other horses were feeding in the pasture.

Minute Man said, "We will wait here."

Lo and behold, the old vampire stepped out of the barn. He walked up to Milo, "Hi, Milo, and how are you on this fine night?"

"Well, Vampire, I am fine. It is a pleasure to meet you."

"Thank you, Milo."

Minute Man said, "Milo, this is the one and only Bugsy."

"Minute Man, I hate it when you call me Bugsy! You should pay your elders more respect! Milo, my name is Horatio. I am almost as old as time. The Top Being created me."

Milo reached out and touched Horatio with his nose.

"Milo, that tickles!" and he began to giggle.

Horatio did not look anything like what Milo had expected. He was not scary looking. He was cute, in his own way. He had no teeth.

"I suppose Minute Man told you about how I lost my teeth?" and he giggled. "Milo, I am old, but my spirit is young. Sometimes I still act like a kid. In fact, most of the time I am that way!"

Milo said, "That is a wonderful way to be! You should never let your spirit get old."

"Oh, Milo, it never has," and he did a back-flip. He jumped on Minute Man and off they went, running across the field.

Horatio hollered out, "Up, up, and away!" and then they were airborne. They flew around the field and over the barn. Horatio was laughing and then he began to sing, "Come fly with me…"

*How wonderful Horatio is! It is a shame that he lost his teeth. It must be really hard for him to eat!*

Milo went and woke up the fairies, "Hey, fairies, would it be possible to help Horatio and pull some magical trick and help him grow some new teeth?"

The fairies put their heads together and began to hum. They stopped and said, "Milo, we are going to give it a go. When Horatio gets back, we will talk it over."

Horatio and Minute Man came flying in. Milo talked to Horatio about new teeth.

He became ecstatic, "New teeth? Milo, do you think that they can pull it off?"

"It could be possible."

The fairies put Horatio in a trance. They opened his mouth and went to work. (The fairies were wonderful at everything! That's why Milo was so beautiful and that was why he could sing so well.) Horatio's teeth would be perfect!

When they finished, they told Milo to watch over him. "Wake him just before dawn." So Milo stood over him the rest of the night. Milo thought about how Horatio had been around since the beginning of time. He must have a huge amount of knowledge stored in his mind. *I wonder if he knows the story about "The Tortoise and the Hare."*

Milo laughed. A special feeling radiated from Horatio. Milo said, "This is the BEST of the BEST of the BEST!"

Mhilo came over and kept Milo company through the night. They talked about life and how wonderful it could be, if everyone lived by the virtues. Milo told Mhilo about Inferno and what a majestic horse he was. He told him about Justice and then he touched Mhilo. He said, "You are a very special horse sent here to take care of the farm and watch over the other horses. Mhilo, the Holy Cow considers you to be one of the special horses of the world. You will be rewarded."

Mhilo bowed his head and a special feeling of serenity came over him.

It was time to wake Horatio. Milo gave him a nudge with his hoof.

Horatio yawned and awoke. He stood up and spoke. His voice sounded different because of his new teeth. He reached up and touched them. "Teeth! Wonderful teeth!" Horatio giggled, "Oh, thank you! Thank you! Thank you! How do I look, Milo?"

"Oh, you are very handsome, Vampire Horatio." And they both laughed.

Milo said, "Let's go try your new teeth,"

Milo and Horatio went into the barn. They opened the oat barrel and they both ate.

Milo said, "I love oats!"

"I love them too," Horatio said. "I will never have to eat bugs again!" And he smiled a huge smile. His new teeth glistened pearly white.

He looked at Milo. "Milo, you will go to the state of Texas. The Holy Cow told me to tell you."

*Texas...why Texas?*

So Milo and the fairies said their goodbyes.

The fairies headed south, "Texas, here we come!"

Milo and the fairies walked along.

Guess who came flying by? It was Mr. Cool, the pileated woodpecker! He lit on a dead balsam tree.

"Hello, Milo, it has been awhile."

"Mr. Cool, it is great to see you. What's new?"

"Well, Milo, the winter was a cold one."

"Yes, Mr. Cool, Breaker told me all about it," and Milo shivered.

Mr. Cool laughed, "Winter, spring, summer, fall—I love the seasons! I love them all. Milo, there are some newly dead trees in the forest. Soon they will be full of bugs and worms. Mother Nature seems to always take care of us. I hate to see some of the trees die, but it is part of the ecosystem. Some things must die, so other things can live. It is part of the Top Being's grand design. Well, Milo, I must move on."

Mr. Cool pecked the dead balsam. The chips flew; he pulled out a worm, and flew off. He would share it with his family. Sharing is the GREATEST of the GREATEST!

(I fooled you! I left out one of the GREATESTs. Oh, I forgot to tell you…Milo asked the old Vampire Horatio about 'The Tortoise and the Hare.' Horatio told Milo the story. Milo would be ready for the race that was to come. He would not make the same mistake the hare did. He would not underestimate the turtle. It would be the race of a lifetime.) Milo thought, *Would it be possible that the turtle could fly? She is shaped like a flying saucer.* (How did Milo know about flying saucers? Ashlee the Star Girl told Milo about them. She had seen flying saucers in her dimension.)

Milo, the fairies, Raven, and Vulture moved on. It would be a long walk from Minnesota to Texas.

Milo said, "I am tired!"

"Okay, Milo, we will sleep in the Minnesota forest." They pulled the *Blanket of Sparkling Mist* over Milo and went to sleep.

Milo awoke early, it was just breaking light. Milo looked around. There were no fairies in sight.

Milo called out, "Fairies! Fairies, where are you?"

"We are right behind you."

Milo turned around. There was a cloud of fuzz floating in the air. "Fairies, Fairies, where are you?"

"Milo, the cloud of fuzz is us."

"What? You have got to be kidding!"

"No, Milo, we never kid. Milo, we have never told you we can take on many life forms. This is one of them. Look closely at us, Milo." They flew right around Milo's eyes.

Milo could see they were tiny flies. Their bodies were light purple. Their wings were round in shape.

Their tails were white and fuzzy—that is why they looked like fuzz floating in the air.

The small fairies in their new life-form were beautiful. They were a little less than a quarter-inch in length.

Milo said, "If you wouldn't have spoken to me, I would have thought you were just little puffs of fuzz."

The fairies laughed. They said, "Milo, close your eyes."

Milo closed his eyes.

"Now open them," and there the fairies were in their regular form.

Milo said, "That was unbelievable!"

"Oh, Milo, you ain't seen nothing yet!"

Milo laughed. The fairies laughed. It was a wonderful time in their lives. And the best part of it was their lives would go on…FOREVER!

The fairies said, "Milo, we are going to Texas by air." They picked Milo up and flew him to Texas (Milo was a little apprehensive about flight, but he trusted the fairies). It did not take too long, only one day, and they were in Texas.

They set Milo down on the Texas border. Milo took one step and he was in Texas!

## CHAPTER 30 | **PALO DURO CANYON**

Milo traveled to Palo Duro Canyon. Milo looked around, he felt uneasy. "Fairies, Raven, Vulture, what do you feel like?"

They all spoke at once, "Uneasy and tense. There is something wrong with this place. Something sinister happened here, Milo."

Just then, a majestic lightning bolt split the clear blue sky wide open, and from out of the split came a horse at full gallop. The horse hit the ground right in front of Milo.

Milo jumped back. The horse was an Akhal-Teke. "Hello, Milo, Raven, Vulture, fairies, it is a pleasure to meet you all."

Milo and everyone were so startled they could hardly speak, but they got the words out nevertheless. "Hi…Hi…Hi…Hi." They were all shaking.

"Do not be afraid."

The Arch Fairies, Joan and Mika, flew to the horse and gently touched the horse's cheeks. They spoke, "This is an angel horse, Milo."

"Yes, Milo, I am an angel horse. I have been sent to you by the Top Being. I will explain to you all that happened here on these grounds."

The angel horse bowed her head, "Milo, one thousand forty-eight horses died here. They were killed by humans. And then, 200 miles from here, six to seven thousand more horses were also killed by humans."

Milo said, "How could they do that to us?" He started to cry and then he stomped his feet. Rage filled his body. His eyes bulged, and they glowed red. He stomped the ground so hard, the ground shook. He kicked with both feet at once.

The fairies hollered out, "MILO, CALM DOWN! Calm down!"

Milo shook with rage. The fairies touched Milo gently, and Milo's rage began to subside.

Milo spoke, "Angel Horse, how could they do that to us?"

"Milo, they do that to each other. It is called genocide. They slaughter each other in the same way."

Milo said, "I will summon my brother Inferno, and we will take revenge on those humans. We will make them pay. We will stomp them into the dirt. We will kick them into the middle of next week. We will end their lives!"

A huge black cloud instantly formed in the sky. A voice came from the cloud, it was the voice of the Top Being, "Milo, cease! For vengeance is mine only. The matter has been taken care of." And the cloud disappeared.

It was hard for Milo to give up the thought of vengeance. It seemed to linger in his mind.

*The Top Being told me to drop it, let it go. In other words, don't go there, Milo. Don't even think about it!*

Milo shook his head and the thought left his mind.

He looked at the Akhal-Teke. He walked over to her. He put his nose on her and smelled her. *She smells heavenly!* Milo thought, *Why did the word "heavenly" come into this sentence?*

Akhal-Teke spoke, "Milo, I put the word 'heavenly' into this story because angel horses come from Horse Heaven. We do not come from the Special Place. We come from Horse Heaven; all horses that are killed by genocide go there."

Milo said, "Oh, how wonderful!"

"Milo, I want to talk about the good things in the Universe. Angel horses have a very special gift. We are able to change. We can look any way you want us to look. We can be any color you want us to be, any size, any disposition. You see, Milo, we were created for everyone that loves horses."

A special feeling came over Milo. He laughed, "This is the BEST of the BEST of the BEST!"

Milo felt like someone was watching him from behind. He spun around and, lo and behold, there stood Inferno.

"You summoned me, Milo? What can I do for you?"

"Inferno, I was thinking about vengeance, but I have changed my mind."

"Milo, you have made the right decision. For you and I could destroy the human race. It would be the ultimate genocide. But it would damn us forever and then this story would end."

Milo thought, *Inferno used the word "damn," it must have two meanings!*

Everyone was happy to see Inferno.

Milo spoke, "Inferno, I want you to meet this horse from heaven."

Milo turned around and the Akhal-Teke was gone! (While Milo was talking to Inferno, she had walked away across the Universe.)

Milo said, "She is gone!"

Inferno said, "Was she an Akhal-Teke?"

"Yes, Inferno, and she smelled heavenly."

"Yes, Milo all horses from heaven smell that way. You see, Milo, I know all the horses in Horse Heaven."

"How do you know all of them, Inferno?"

"Well, Milo, I escorted all of them to heaven. They followed me across the Universe. It was a sight to behold! It made the Top Being cry."

Milo said, "What a wonderful thing you did, Inferno!"

"Thank you, Milo."

"How are Azura and the children?"

"They are fine. I left them at Mirror Lake. They love the apple tree."

"Yes, Inferno, I have got to say those apples are the BEST!" Milo laughed, "I forgot to put the other two BESTS into the sentence."

Inferno laughed, "Milo, you are a real character! Hey, Milo, I ran into George and Justice. They said, 'Hi.' That George is quite a horseman. Justice and I talked about the cavalry. He is a Marwari Horse. When I was in the cavalry, what brave, loyal horses they were! Well, Milo, I must get back to my family."

Inferno trotted away and slowly disappeared.

The fairies said, "Milo, we must move out."

Milo said, "No, we will stay here for the night. I want some answers."

"Okay, Milo, let's talk."

"Fairies, whose horses were they?"

"They were Indians' horses."

"Indians' horses?"

"Yes, Milo, the Indians were humans. They lived in North America. They occupied the land before the white humans came. The white humans moved into the lands. The Indian humans and the white humans could not get along. So, like humans do, they started to kill each other."

Milo said, "Humans are a strange species! They always resort to domination and, if that doesn't work, they kill each other. War seems to be their destiny. So why do they kill the animal species?"

"They are crazy, Milo. Eventually, they will destroy the world. That is why we were sent here. Milo, we must try to save the world with faith, hope, love, and charity. We must get the humans to change their ways."

Milo said, "Do you think it is possible?"

"Yes, Milo, anything is possible. Never lose hope, Milo. Never give up. Be optimistic, it can be done. Faith, hope, love, and charity are slowly spreading across the world."

Milo said, "Yes, humans would not have made it without us, and now us horses will save mankind. Dang, we truly are the BEST of the BEST of the BEST!" Milo reared up. He let out that huge whinny of his, and it echoed around the world and across the Universe.

The Top Being stood up and whinnied back, and it echoed around the world. The humans cowered as they heard the whinnies. (Yes, my friends, the Top Being had pure horse blood in his veins. The humans in the world would come to their knees someday, and the world would be saved.)

Milo thought how if only he could have been around when horses were introduced to the Indian humans and the white humans, it was possible things could have turned out differently. Maybe he could have made peace between the humans and saved the lives of the horses and the humans. They were such different species and they had such different views on nature. But if they would have had faith, hope, love, and charity, they would have been able to enter into brotherhood, and peacefulness would have prevailed.

The white humans' world was totally different. Their world was about taking, about dominance and money, the root of all evil. The whites' government was based on money. Money came first, Top Being second, nature last, so this made brotherhood impossible for the Indians and the whites. The Indians loved the world the Top Being had given them. Everything in nature meant something special to them: animals, water, plants, sun and their creator. The Top Being came first.

The fairies touched Milo gently and comforted him. The Holy Cow and the Top Being sprinkled Milo with a holy dust; its sparkles filled the air.

The fairies covered Milo with the *Blanket of Sparkling Mist* and Milo slept.

Vulture and Raven were totally silent through the whole ordeal. They felt Milo's sorrow. They loved Milo with all their hearts and all their minds and all their souls. Milo was their brother, brother, brother.

When morning came, Milo awoke. He rose to his feet. The sun was breaking the horizon. The sunlight shone on Milo. He looked magnificent. The Indian horse spirits had come during the night. They had painted Milo the same way the Indians had painted them to record their bravery in battle.

The fairies, Raven, and Vulture stood and marveled at the way Milo looked, and then they sang the song from the Special Place. When the song was finished, the fairies said, "Milo, we must move out."

CHAPTER 31 | **TRAVELING THE STATES**

So Milo and the team walked the border between Texas and Mexico. They spread the word of faith, hope, love, and charity. Milo touched everyone with his nose, and brotherhood began to spread throughout Texas.

They turned north and walked through the middle of Texas; they were headed for Montana.

Milo loved the humans of Texas. *These are wonderful humans!*

The fairies said, "Milo, we are going to walk the state lines between New Mexico and Oklahoma and Kansas and Colorado, Nebraska, and Wyoming, South Dakota and Wyoming, South Dakota, and North Dakota and Montana."

They headed for Crow Agency, Montana.

They arrived early in the morning. The sun was just breaking the horizon. Milo walked amongst the horses at the Crow Fair. Milo talked to the horses that had lived since the year 1529. (The humans did not know this. The Top Being had tricked their minds.) The horses were so beautiful, and their history was unbelievable.

Milo loved speaking with them. There were horses of all kinds—different colors, different breeds. They were tough horses. (They had to be because of the tough events they would compete in.)

The horses talked to Milo. They told him about the relay race, about calf roping, team roping, saddle-bronc riding, and track racing. The humans that rode these horses were "Tough, tough, tough" (as Frog would say)—they had to be, because their horses were super tough.

Milo thought, *I will run with these horses. It will be a blast!* So Milo ran with the horses. When all the events were over, the humans talked about the Buckskin Paint Horse that was competing without a rider. They thought that maybe his rider had fallen off. Some humans said the Buckskin Paint never had a rider, he just ran with the other horses.

The humans talked about the singing they had heard. They laughed and said, "It must have been our imagination." Some of the humans said, "That Buckskin Paint ran right alongside me and, believe me, he was singing!"

Everyone laughed, and then the singing began again. Everyone looked toward the sound and, lo and behold, a singing Buckskin Paint trotted off into the sunset. A raven and a vulture flew above the Paint.

The humans and their horses could not believe what they had just seen and heard. They all bowed their heads and stood silently, and a feeling of brotherhood swept over them. It was a special time in their lives, a time they would never forget.

Milo, the fairies, Raven, and Vulture headed for Omak, Washington. They would go to the Omak Stampede. Milo had heard about the "Suicide Race" and he wanted to race in it.

Milo walked into Omak around noon. The horses and riders were busy. They did not notice the Buckskin Paint, he blended in perfectly. Night came. The riders were readying themselves and their horses for the race.

All of a sudden, a young girl jumped on Milo's back. "Hello, Milo Boy, do you remember me?" It was Ashlee the Star Girl.

Milo was so startled, he could not speak.

"Milo, the elders sent me here to ride you in the Suicide Race."

"Ashlee, it is so good to see you. Ashlee, I got your message that you wrote in the sky, it truly touched my heart." Milo began to laugh, and Ashlee laughed with him.

The race was about to start. Ashlee snapped her fingers and her helmet appeared. She put the helmet on and tightened the chinstrap.

Milo walked to the starting line. He would race against the tough horses. Milo had a smile on his face. He said a short prayer, "Holy Cow, protect my brothers," and the race began.

Milo reached the sixty-two-degree slope. He plunged down the slope and dove into the Okanogan River, swam the river, ran up the bank, galloped into the arena, and crossed the finish line!

The crowd was silent. They could not believe what they had just seen. Milo had broken the record time by thirty seconds!

The Vulture swooped down, grabbed the microphone from the announcer. "The winner is Milo! The rider is Ashlee! You ain't seen nothing yet!"

The crowd roared. A shooting star swooped down from the night sky; it picked Ashlee up, and flew away. The crowd was awestruck.

Milo jumped the arena fence and disappeared into the night.

Milo and everyone headed for Oregon. They would go to the Pendleton Round-Up.

(Well, folks, I have brought the star girl, Ashlee, back into the Milo story for a good reason. She is one of the few humans qualified to ride Milo in a dangerous race like the Suicide Race. The Star Dimension and the Star Humans are quite intriguing. Milo will go to the Star Dimension in time. Folks, you ain't seen nothing yet!)

Milo was tired. It was time to rest. The fairies pulled the *Blanket of Sparkling Mist* over Milo.

Before Milo fell asleep, he talked to the Top Being. He asked him to bless the state of Washington.

The Top Being smiled, "Oh, Milo, you never forget your brothers. I am so proud of you!" The Top Being held his hands over Washington and sprinkled the state with his Blessed Dust.

It was done!

## CHAPTER 32 | **THE COLUMBIA RIVER**

Milo fell asleep. He dreamed about the beavers in Minnesota. They were such fun!

It was morning. The fairies pulled Milo's ears.

He shook his head. *Damn, I hate that!* Milo thought. *I wonder why I said the word "damn"? I sure do like that word.* He chuckled.

Raven and Vulture flew in. "Good morning, Milo, it sure is a damn fine morning!" And they all laughed.

The fairies scolded them. "You guys, should not speak that way!"

Vulture laughed, "Oh, now-now, little miss perfects!" And he laughed again.

Mika and Joan rushed toward Vulture. Vulture took off. Mika and Joan chased Vulture through the air. They caught him and brought him back to Milo.

Vulture broke loose from their grasp. He hopped between Milo's legs. "Now, ladies, ease up! Vulture was just kidding," Milo said.

"No, I was not kidding, Milo. They do think they are perfect!"

"That's enough, Vulture! Ease up, Mika and Joan! It is time to go to Oregon."

Everyone calmed down. But Milo could tell the animosity between them was not over. He thought, *Damn, that was fun to watch!* He chuckled.

Milo and everyone walked toward Oregon. They came to a huge river.

Vulture flew in, "Milo, it's the Columbia River!"

Milo walked down the bank of the river. He put his head down and smelled the water. "I have never smelled water that smells this way."

Vulture smelled the water. "It smells like some kind of fish to me."

"Fish," Milo said. "Fish, what do you mean?"

"Fish, Milo, they live in the water."

"How do they breathe?"

"They pull oxygen out of the water."

Milo said, "This is really confusing. 'Fish,' 'oxygen,' I don't get it. Sounds kind of 'fishy' to me."

Just then a huge salmon jumped out of the water. When it came down, it splashed water on Milo. He jumped back. The huge salmon circled around and came back to Milo.

The fish spoke, "And what species are you?"

"I am a horse. What species are you?"

"I am a fish."

Milo said, "You have no legs!"

"I don't need legs. I have a tail." He showed Milo his tail.

Milo said, "I have a tail. It's to keep the bugs off of me."

The fish laughed at Milo's tail.

Milo said, "We are so different in every way!"

"Yes, horse, the Top Being created us to live in water."

"I know the Top Being."

"Horse, everyone and everything knows the Top Being. He created everything."

Just then, a huge fish swam up to the salmon and to Milo. The fish was eight feet long! "Hello, Milo!"

"How do you know my name?"

"Milo, I am a sturgeon. I have been around since time began. I have been given a special gift. I can read your mind and, Milo, you sure do have a wonderful mind!"

"Thank you, Sturgeon."

A small fish swam up to Milo. It was a walleye. His eyes were large, and he had "stickers" on the end of his fins. He laughed when he looked at Milo, "Boy, you sure are strange looking!"

"Yes, fish, we sure are different in every way. You have been created for water, and I have been created for land." They both laughed.

"Come swim with us, Milo."

Milo jumped into the water and began to swim.

The fish dove under the water. Milo took a deep breath; he filled his lungs with air, and dove under. Milo could not believe that he could actually see underwater. It was strange!

The fish swam along with Milo. Milo couldn't believe how fast they could swim!

Milo thought, "I do not think I can swim as fast as the fish, but I will give it a try." Milo tried to make himself as sleek as possible. He stretched his neck out, he stuck his tall out, and he pulled his feet and legs up closer to his body, and began to paddle as fast as possible.

His speed increased immensely, but he could not swim as fast as the fish. He was running out of air. He would have to surface, so up he went. He broke the surface. Milo took a deep breath.

The fish surfaced, "Milo, you did quite well! We are surprised."

Milo said, "I gave it all I had. That is the best I can do underwater. Yes, fish, as you can see, I surely cannot swim as fast as you can!"

"Milo, what is important is you tried hard! You put everything into it; you were not a slacker."

It was a great day for Milo and the fish. They became brothers.

Milo stepped on shore. He was in Oregon.

Milo walked up the bank of the river. He heard a roaring sound. "What is that?"

Raven and Vulture said, "We will fly ahead and check it out."

Soon they were back. "Milo, it's a waterfall! Come with us."

Milo thought, "A waterfall. Never have I heard of a waterfall." Milo walked along the bottom of a high bluff. He rounded a corner, and there it was.

The water came cascading from above. Milo looked up, the waterfall was so high. It made Milo dizzy as he watched the water break over the top and come tumbling down. The mist from the falls made Milo's hair glisten in the sunlight.

"What a masterpiece that Milo Boy is," said the fairies. They flew from Milo's mane. The light they gave off sparkled in the mist.

Vulture and Raven flew to the top of the falls. They looked toward Washington and up the river; there was a huge dam that crossed the river. They said, "We have to show Milo that dam. We will not tell him about it. It will be fun to see how he reacts when he sees it!"

They flew back to Milo. "Hey, Milo, let's walk upstream."

So Milo, Raven, Vulture, and the fairies walked along. Milo began to sing as he walked. His voice was beautiful, it echoed off the canyon walls. All of a sudden, he came to an abrupt halt. His eyes focused on the huge dam that crossed the river.

"What is that?"

"It's a dam, Milo."

"Did beavers build that?"

"No, Milo, humans built that dam."

"Damn, that's the biggest dam I have ever seen." Milo began to laugh. His laugh echoed off the canyon walls.

The fairies flew from Milo's mane and they began to sing. "Oh, Milo Boy, oh, Milo Boy, as you can plainly see that is a dam. Damn that makes electricity, yes, siree."

They laughed. The word "damn" was starting to rub off on them. They wouldn't admit it, but they liked saying that "damn" word.

Raven and Vulture pointed at them. "Shame on you, fairies, you should not say that 'damn' word!"

The Fairies flew at Vulture and Raven. They pulled a feather out of each one of them.

It hurt when the fairies pulled their feathers! They hollered out.

And then they began to laugh, it was a grand time in their lives. It was a fun time! It was a time to laugh and a time to smile. Joy is the BEST of the BEST of the BEST!

## CHAPTER 33 | **PENDLETON ROUND-UP**

Milo and the team headed for the Pendleton Round-Up in Pendleton, Oregon. Milo would race in the ladies' bareback race. He would have to find a rider. She would have to be a skilled bareback rider.

Milo walked into Pendleton; it was early in the morning. He found the rodeo grounds. He walked amongst the horses. There were horses that dated back as far as 1519. Sorraia, Barb, Spanish Jennet, American Quarter Horse, Appaloosa, and many other breeds.

There were horses from 1519 to 2018. (The humans did not know this because the Top Being had, once again, tricked their minds.)

A beautiful Indian girl stood with her horse. Her name was Destiny. The horse's name was Buck.

The place was crowded with horses and humans. Milo walked up to a girl; she had her back to Milo. Milo thought, *I have smelled this human before....* He bumped her with his nose.

She spun around. It was Jessica! "Is it you, Milo?"

"Oh, yes, Jessica!"

"Oh, Milo, it is so good to see you. I think about you every day!"

Milo responded, "Likewise. Jessica, I have come here to race in the ladies' bareback race. I am looking for a rider."

"I will ride you, Milo, and we will win!"

Milo laughed, "Oh, Jessica, don't be so sure. You could fall off."

"Yes, Milo, anything can happen, but it will be so much fun." Jessica laughed. She gave Milo a big hug.

Milo thought, *This woman really fits into the world. The world is a better place because of Jessica.*

Jessica got on Milo's back. She put her hand on Milo's withers. She could feel the tremendous power in his body.

Milo said, "Jessica, are you ready?"

"Yes, Milo."

And Milo walked onto the racetrack. The horses on the track were beautiful, and the women were beautiful. The horses all had smiles on their faces; they loved to race.

The riders noticed that Milo had no bridle. "Your horse has no bridle."

Jessica spoke. "I control my horse with leg and heel and toe pressure."

*Oh, Jessica, you just told a fib.*

(You see, Milo did not need any guidance. All Jessica had to do was hang on.)

The horses trotted toward the starting line, and the race began. A huge burst of energy filled the air. Milo held back, he was in fourth place. Slowly, he increased his speed—third place, second place. He ran stride for stride with the horse in first place. They rounded the corner and entered the straightaway.

Jessica was silent. She heard the other rider talking to her horse, "Go, June, Go!" (She had named her horse June. It was the month they were both born in.) Her horse June was a blue roan.

She was a beautiful woman. Her name was Mia.

She had a smile on her face. Her smile was heavenly. Her hair was black and was in braids. She wore a long-sleeve shirt. The sleeves were decorated with gold braiding.

Milo thought, *I will let June win.*

Then Holy Cow spoke to Milo. "Milo, you must win this race, it is your destiny."

Milo pulled ahead of June half a length and crossed the finish line. Tears formed in Milo's eyes. He was not happy that he had won.

June trotted up to Milo, "Milo, why are you crying?"

"I am so sorry, June."

"Oh, Milo, do not be that way."

"June, you know my name?"

"Yes, Milo, I was sent here by the Holy Cow to race you. It was a test, Milo. She wanted to see if you would obey her command."

Milo said, "I have a question for you, June."

"What is the question, Milo?"

"Were you running at full speed?"

"Oh, no, Milo, I was running at one-quarter speed." June started to laugh; it was a beautiful laugh, it was an angel's laugh.

Milo smiled. Milo had a vision at that moment. The vision was June and him racing across the Universe.

When the vision was gone, Milo looked around. June was nowhere in sight.

Jessica had witnessed and heard the whole conversation. Jessica laughed, "Milo, do you think you can outrun June?"

Milo hesitated.

Jessica slapped Milo on the neck.

Milo quit hesitating. *Jessica, I will stomp June,* Milo thought. *Well, maybe.* Milo reared up and let out a huge whinny.

Jessica hollered out, "That's my Milo Boy!"

Milo began to sing a horse song.

Milo dropped Jessica off at the old pickup. As Jessica got in the pickup, Milo hollered out, "How is the glove box?"

Jessica gave Milo the "thumbs up" and drove away.

(Well, folks, what do you think? Was June telling Milo the truth about how fast she could run? Or could she run 400 miles an hour across the desert floor? Angel horses were known for telling little fibs.)

Milo, Raven, Vulture, and the fairies headed out. They would look for a portal.

Milo walked along. He came to a large pond. "Fairies, look at the size of this pond!"

"Yes, Milo, it is a duck pond."

"What is a duck?"

Just then, a duck went whizzing by. "Duck, Milo, here comes a duck!"

Milo ducked. The duck almost clipped Milo's ears off. "Wahoo! That was close! I am glad it missed my ears!"

The duck circled and lit in the water. The duck paddled over to Milo and walked up on land. He ran at Milo, his neck stretched out, "Quack! Quack! Quack!"

Milo backed up as the duck ran towards him.

The duck stopped. "What are you, a chicken?"

Milo said, "No, I am a horse."

The duck laughed, "Just kidding."

Milo said, "I have been called a chicken before. Do I look like a chicken?"

"No, you look like a horse."

"Then why do you call me a chicken?" *I wonder what a chicken looks like?*

"Milo, the word 'chicken' is a word that humans use when they think you are afraid, when they think you are a weakling, or when you will not fight back.

"A chicken is a bird, quite small and fluttery. Some male chickens will fight, they are called roosters. They are also good alarm clocks, at the break of dawn they crow loudly. When humans taunt each other, they call each other 'chickens.'"

Milo thought that Minute Man must have learned the "chicken, chicken, chicken" thing from humans. *It is strange. I wonder why it aggravates me. Oh well, I better quit thinking and talking about this subject. I am getting confused.*

"Hey, Duck, you can walk and run on land. You can swim in water, you can swim underwater, and you

can fly. Wow! I have got to say you are real special!"

"Thanks, Milo, a lot of humans never really think about us ducks. And, Milo, do you know that we can sleep with one eye open? The eye that is open watches for danger while the other eye sleeps, and then we turn around and reverse the process."

Milo said, "Boy, that's just 'ducky'!" The duck laughed.

*Now why did I say that? Boy, sometimes strange things happen to me.*

"Well, Milo, see you later." The duck took off.

Milo said, "Boy, those ducks can really fly fast!" (Hey, folks, do some research on how fast a duck can fly!)

## CHAPTER 34 | **THE WHITE PINE DIMENSION**

Milo walked along slowly; his heart was full of joy. He smiled as he thought about his wonderful adventures. He spoke out loud, "Holy Cow, Top Being, what's next? I can't wait!" and he laughed. As I said before, his laugh was beautiful.

Milo sucked in the beautiful fresh air of his Dimension. The air made his huge lungs tingle.

The fairies, Vulture and Raven flew above him! What a sight they were.

Milo looked ahead, and he spotted a small creature waddling along in the distance. Milo broke into a trot, and just before he got to the strange creature, the creature disappeared. The creature had stepped into his own Dimension. He entered the White Pine Dimension.

Milo stopped, he sniffed the air. The scent of the white pine trees made him sneeze! The fairies grabbed the *Blanket of Sparkling Mist* and held it in front of the hole and Milo looked in. And before his eyes appeared a beautiful forest of white pine trees.

Snow covered the ground. Milo had never seen snow. "Fairies, what's the white stuff?"

"It's snow, Milo."

Milo said, "Snow?"

"Yes, Milo, it's frozen moisture."

"Hey fairies, the old cowboy talked about snow. I never did ask him what it was!" and Milo laughed, and he stepped into the White Pine Dimension.

The snow felt cool on Milo's feet, he laughed as he walked in the snow. The creature he was following began to climb a white pine tree. Milo hollered out, "Wait, I want to talk to you." The creature climbed down from the tree; he waddled over to Milo. He spoke; his voice was slow and methodical.

"Howdy horse!"

"You know I am a horse?"

"Yes I have seen a lot of you horses, you horses help log the pine forest."

"We do?"

"Oh yes horse, you skid the pine logs for the humans. Milo, you have stepped back in time."

Milo spoke, "Hey who are you?"

"Well, Milo I am a porcupine."

Milo stepped forward and touched porcupine with his nose. Milo jumped back. Five of the porcupine's quills were stuck in his nose! The pain was intense! The fairies grabbed the quills and pulled them out. Milo rubbed his nose in the snow. The snow relieved the pain. The fairies covered Milo's nose with a cool green mist, it was the same mist they used when Milo was full of bug bites.

Porcupine spoke. "Milo, I was going to warn you about my quills but you were too quick for me." "Milo, I will take you to the logging site, follow me."

So Milo followed Porcupine at his slow pace. Milo thought this porcupine had got to be the slowest creature in the world, and he chuckled inside.

Milo could hear the sound of the loggers' axes and their crosscut saws. The smell of sawdust was in the air. A team of huge horses came along; they were pulling a sleigh full of pine logs on an ice trail. They stopped to talk to Milo. "Hi horse, what are you doing here?"

Milo said, "Oh I just came to the White Pine Dimension from my Dimension. It is great to meet you guys!"

"You sure are a small, slim, trim horse; you would not be of much use here." And the team laughed, and their laughter echoed through the pine trees.

"Hey boys, how much do you each weigh?"

"We weigh 1,850 lbs each."

Milo said, "I know a horse that weighs four-thousand pounds. His name is Inferno."

"We have never seen a horse that large."

Milo asked, "Would you like to meet him?"

"We sure would!"

"I will summon him."

The team of horses began to laugh.

"Get ready because here he comes!"

Milo stomped the ground 4 times and hollered out, "Inferno!" The ground began to tremble, a purple haze filled the air, and a huge grey, black, and purple horse stepped out of the pine trees. It was Inferno! The team of horses could not believe their eyes!

Inferno walked up to Milo and the team of horses. He gave a bow and everyone bowed back. Inferno talked to everyone with his mind, his eyes and his ears, and his body reactions. Everyone did the same. Not a word was spoken. Yes folks, horses communicate that way. You see, actions speak louder than words: a lesson all humans must learn.

This is what Inferno said to the team. "Horses, you have been chosen by the Top Being to drop your harnesses and come with me. I will take you to him." The harnesses fell from their bodies and they walked away with Inferno and disappeared into the pine forest.

Porcupine had hidden behind a huge pine stump and watched the whole episode.

Milo spoke, "Well, Porcupine, what do you think of that?"

"Amazing, Milo, simply amazing!"

"Well, Porcupine, what do you do?"

"I climb the trees and eat the bark off around the tree, it's called girdling, and this causes the tree to die."

"Why do you do this?"

"The Top Being made me this way and I am not about to question him."

"Smart, Porcupine, I never question the Top Being, he has a purpose for everything. Sometimes we just have to except what he hands us."

Milo turned and looked at the fairies, the Raven and the Vulture. "Well, let's move out." Vulture and Raven said that Porcupine was simply one amazing creature.

The mystery of the disappearing team of horses has never been solved. The story has been handed down from generation to generation. But now the mystery is over, thanks to the story of Milo the Legend.

Oh, I forgot to tell you, that the human that was driving the horses was put in a trance by the fairies. He could not remember a thing that had happened. He was not criticized or blamed for what happened that day. Everyone treated him with compassion. You see, there were no tracks in the snow, and the snow around the sleigh had a faint purple tint to it. What happened that day was considered to be a Divine Miracle.

As Frog would say, "Amen, Amen, Amen!"

## CHAPTER 35 | **QUARTER HORSE DIMENSION**

As Milo walked along, his mind wandered back to the time he met Secretariat. Secretariat's story of the human dressed in white with gold trim, with a purple sash, intrigued Milo. *I wonder who that human is?*

The fairies spoke, "Stop, Milo."

A portal appeared right in front of Milo. Milo stepped to his right, the portal moved right. He moved left, the portal moved left.

Milo laughed. *This must be some kind of a game.* No matter what way Milo moved, the portal stayed in front of his nose.

The fairies stretched the *Blanket of Sparkling Mist* over the portal, and Milo stuck his head through the hole.

Milo was looking at a beautiful racetrack. The track had a half-mile straightaway. The side rails glowed a lustrous white. Milo stepped onto the track. The dirt felt good on his feet, it made his legs tingle and his muscles quiver. The air around Milo sparkled with freshness.

He took a deep breath. He began to gallop at a lively pace. Milo heard the thunder of a horse's hooves. He looked behind and there was a herd of horses running at him. A pearl white cloud traveled over them. The horses were a sight to behold! He stopped and turned to face them. They ran by. The energy from their powerful muscles shook the air around Milo. The horses crossed the finish line of the racetrack. They slowed, circled the track and came back.

They trotted up to Milo and came to a stop. A horse by the name Traveler, spoke, "Hello, Milo, we were expecting you."

"You know me?"

"Yes, Milo, we sure do! You are the Paint Horse that will change the world!"

The horses stepped forward one at a time and spoke their names. "Traveler…Old Joe Bailey…Lucky Blanton…Peter McCue…Midnight…Midnight Jr…Grey Badger II…Skipper W…Oklahoma Star… Oklahoma Star Jr…Driftwood…Jessie James…King's Pistol…My Texas Dandy…Clabber…Rocket Bar… Lightning Bar…Sugar Bars…Moon Deck…Jet Deck…Lena's Bar…Easy Jet."

The horses spoke, "There are more of us, but it is our day to run." The horses circled Milo, it was a wonderful sight! They hollered out, "Hip-Hip-Hooray!" three times and, one by one, they trotted away.

As they trotted away, Milo noticed there was something silver on their hooves.

One horse stayed. It was Jet Deck. Jet Deck was magnificent! The fairies ran Jet Deck's statistics through Milo's mind.

Milo spoke, "Jet Deck, you truly are one of the BEST of the BEST horses to have walked on the face of the earth! Jet Deck I have a question for you."

"What is the question Milo? "

"Let me look at your hooves."

Jet Deck showed Milo his hooves. Every hoof had a beautiful silver horseshoe on it.

"What are they for Jet Deck?"

"They protect our hooves and they give us traction."

"Who puts them on your hooves?"

"A human from the world dimension comes here and takes care of our hooves. He trims our hooves and puts these silver shoes on us. He is called a Farrier. Milo, we horses that come from the world have to have our hooves taken care of. Milo, you are one of the special horses that does not have to have this done."

"Jet Deck, who is this human?"

"Milo, his name is Eldon. We call him Butch."

"Oh, a nickname."

"Yes Milo."

Jet Deck and Milo laughed.

"Milo, Butch trims and shoes horses in the world."

"Well how does he have time to come here?"

"Milo, Butch has a spirit. All humans have a spirit. Butch's spirit does this for him."

"Does Butch know his spirit?"

"Well, he might, but if he does know his spirit, he would never tell anyone he did. It is a secret that humans never talk about. You see Milo, Butch is a very special person. Farriers are very special people; they have been given a special gift."

"Who gave them this gift?"

"Oh Milo, the Top Being gave this gift to each and every one of them. Butch also watches our physical condition. He makes us walk and trot around him; he is looking for sore muscles. Butch tells us when it's time to rest and let our muscles repair themselves. Milo, Butch even scratches us, it really feels good! Have you ever had a human scratch you?"

"Yes, Jet Deck, a human named Jessica and a human named Carla have scratched me, they both have ridden me. Ashlee the Star Girl has ridden me but never scratches me. Ashlee is kind of a little smart aleck." Milo and Jet Deck laughed.

"Milo, I have been chosen to warn you about humans. Milo, I loved humans. I trusted them. Never did I think humans would kill me, but they did. They came in the night. They injected me with a poison, and I died."

The thought of revenge entered Milo's mind. His muscles began to quiver. His eyes glowed red. Jet Deck spoke, "Stop right now, Milo! I know what you are thinking. The Top Being has taken care of the matter."

"How do you know this, Jet Deck?"

"The Top Being has shown these humans to me. Yes, Milo…Palo Duro Canyon, Fort Sill, and all the other killings. These humans walk through the Land of Nothing. The air is hot and humid. They are never allowed to rest. Sweat drips from their wretched bodies. They are looking for a way out that they will never find. Amen! Milo, when you are in the world, never travel alone. Keep the fairies with you; they are truly your guardians. They will protect you from all evil." Jet Deck reared up and let out a huge whinny and disappeared.

Milo walked the sacred racetrack. He sang a beautiful song for every horse that had walked on the face of the earth. When the song was finished, Milo spoke those famous words, "We are the BEST of t he BEST of the BEST and we all have four legs and we will save the world! And as Frog would say, 'Amen, amen, amen.' "

Vulture and Raven had watched the whole episode from above. They flew to Milo.

Milo spoke, "Vulture, Raven, what dimension is this?"

"Milo, this is the Quarter Horse Dimension. This dimension is one of the most beautiful dimensions in existence. It is so mystical it will take your breath away."

Milo spoke, "Vulture, Raven, that beautiful cloud that traveled above the horses…was that neat or what?"

"Yes, Milo, the Top Being, the Holy Cow, and the Human dressed in white, gold, and purple were in that cloud. They love watching the horses race."

Milo spoke, "I wonder if they wager on who will win?" and he laughed.

Vulture spoke, "Yes, Milo, they wager on who will win. They are very competitive. They love competition. Remember when the Holy Cow told you she loves competition?"

Milo laughed. He loved the Holy Cow. "And what do they wager on?"

"They wager on who will get to create the next star, the next dimension, or who will get to create the next horse on earth. Milo, they love everything and everyone with an unconditional love."

Milo smiled. He thought, *So no one ever has to feel unloved. They will always be there for them.*

Vulture spoke, "Milo, this dimension will strengthen your faith and purpose, and you will become a better horse."

So Milo traveled through the Quarter Horse Dimension. He met all the Quarter Horses. It was done. Milo and the "brothers" walked along. It was a beautiful night. The clouds were drifting on high, they covered the moon and, then, the moon became uncovered. It was as if the moon and the clouds were playing a game with each other.

Vulture and Raven laid on Milo's back and watched the game the clouds and the moon were playing. Milo's Shadow came and went. The fairies were lying on Milo's neck. Joan and Mika stood between Milo's ears; they hummed a quiet, little song. Peace and tranquility radiated from all of them.

## CHAPTER 36 | **THE TREE**

Milo was in his own Dimension, Milo was walking in uncharted territory.

Milo's mind was having a great time; his mind was singing and laughing, he was so happy that he was a horse! He jumped into the air, he cantered and trotted and galloped, he paced, he sidestepped, he was so quick on his feet, and his speed was unbelievable.

The fairies flew above him. Raven and Vulture circled in the sky above Milo.

Oh yes, have you ever let your mind go nuts with happiness? It is the BEST of the BEST of the BEST!

Milo and his brothers had never been in this part of the Dimension before, it was so different from any place they had ever traveled in. There were streams of multi-colored water flowing in all directions; the ground was firm and moist. Milo splashed through the water. Milo looked ahead; he could see geysers of water shooting out of the ground and into the beautiful fresh air of his Dimension! Milo dodged back and forth through the geysers.

Milo came to a stop, he let out a huge whinny, it echoed across the land. To his surprise, a huge whinny came rolling back to him. The whinny was beautiful; it had various tones in it. Milo thought, *That was incredible! That sounded totally different from my whinny.* Vulture and Raven flew in and landed in front of Milo.

"Milo that was beautiful!"

"That was not me, it came from far away!"

"Whinny again Milo!" So Milo whinnied and a whinny came rolling back. It sounded totally different from Milo's whinny.

They all spoke at once. Amazing, totally amazing. Yes, the porcupine's statement had really made an impression on all of them!

Everyone became silent. "Get ready, I will whinny, and listen to where the sound comes from." So Milo whinnied softly and a whinny came back softly. "Did you get a fix on that?"

"Yes, Milo we sure did! Follow us."

Raven and Vulture took off. The fairies rode on their backs. They flew in an easterly direction, and Milo followed them.

The colored water that was flowing in all directions began to flow to the east, and it formed into a beautiful river. A voice came rolling in. "Boys and girls, follow the river."

Raven, Vulture and the fairies flew in. "Milo, there is a huge pinnacle, it reaches so high into the sky we cannot see its top!"

Milo broke into a gallop headed straight east. He galloped along a riverbank. The colored water was beautiful! Milo could make out an object in the distance, it looked like a mountain that looked like a tree and it looked like a tree that looked like a mountain. Milo headed right for it; soon he was one mile away. It's a tree, no it's a mountain! The river flowed up to its base and disappeared. Milo walked up to it.

"What is it Milo?"

"I don't kno..." and then it spoke!

"I am a tree!"

The tree's voice was pleasant sounding; "Yes I am a tree. My base is one mile in diameter."

Milo was speechless.

"I have a story to tell you all." So the tree began its story.

"The Top Being created a vampire right around the beginning of time. The Vampire was a very happy soul, he was always laughing and singing, and he loved to do backflips. Yes, Milo, and you know a Vampire that laughs and sings and smiles and does backflips, and his name is Horatio."

"Yes, I surely do."

"Well Milo, they are one in the same, Yes, Milo, the Vampire has been around since the beginning of time.

"Tree, you know my name!"

"Oh yes Milo, everyone in this dimension knows your name."

"Milo, the Top Being gave the Vampire a small tree and he told him to plant it where ever he liked, so off he went, singing and skipping along, when all of a sudden he stopped! He dug a small hole and planted the tree. He made sure the roots were pointing down. A small stream appeared. It was only one-quarter inch wide, the water was colored, it flowed to the tree and disappeared. The tree began to grow, and the water continued to flow, and as the tree grew the stream kept getting bigger! Yes Milo, that is how I was created.

"The Vampire skipped away. He skipped for one half mile and fifty feet. He stopped and took a small granite stone from his pocket; it was colored gray, black, and purple. He set the stone on the ground very carefully. The little stone radiated a slight purple haze. Each year the stone and I got bigger. When my base got within fifty feet of the stone, the stone and I quit growing. The stone now weighed 4,000 pounds, and it was colored gray, black, and purple. A purple haze swirled around it.

"One day a human came walking along, he was dressed in a white robe. The robe was trimmed in gold, he wore a purple sash. The human walked up to the stone and laid his hands on the stone. The stone turned into a magnificent horse.

"The horse let out a huge whinny. The human spoke. 'Horse, your name will be Inferno and you will live forever!'

"The human turned and walked away and rose into the sky and disappeared.  The horse Inferno taught me everything, he left nothing out, and then he trotted away. Yes, Milo, I am the tree of  knowledge. Yes, Milo, Inferno even taught me how to whinny.  Milo, Inferno will be your brother forever. The Top Being has given you the perfect gift."

Milo bowed his head; gratefulness entered his mind and his soul.  Milo lifted his head. "Tree, how tall are you?"

"Milo, I am as tall as you want me to be. Milo, use your imagination for imagining things, it is good for everyone!"

"Now Milo, it is time for me to teach you everything. I will be your teacher. Milo, remember when Bravo told you about Theresa?"

"Yes, I surely do!"

"Milo, Theresa is a teacher, she teaches human children, and she has dedicated her life to teaching."

"Tree, what a wonderful thing to do!"

"Yes, Milo, for as the Frog would say, 'Teachers, Teachers, Teachers are Great, Great, Great.'"

"You know Frog?"

"Yes Milo, Frog has been around for ever ever ever."

Milo laughed and then tree sang a little song for all the teachers in the world.

Milo, Fairies, Raven and Vulture hollered out! "Hip-Hip-Hooray!"  The gang all sat down next to the tree and the tree began to teach.

Raven raised his wing. "Yes, Raven?"

"Can I go to the bathroom?"

"Yes, Raven."

So away he went.  Everyone rolled their eyes.

Raven returned. The tree began to teach.

Vulture raised his wing. "Yes, Vulture?"

"Can I go to the bathroom?"

"Yes, Vulture."  Everyone rolled their eyes,

Vulture returned.

The tree began to teach.

The fairies started laughing. They were making faces at each other. The Tree spoke, "That's enough! You can all leave! Milo, you stay.  You trouble makers, move away!  Milo, put your head against me."

The tree instantly transferred all its knowledge into Milo's mind, and it was over.

"Tree, is it alright if I rub my butt on you? It's itchy."

The Tree laughed, "Go ahead." So Milo rubbed his butt on Tree.

*I wonder if there are any Pileated Woodpeckers in the area ...*

"Hey Tree, do you know any woodpeckers?"

"I sure do! There is one that visits me every day. He weighs 150 lbs; his name is Jack, last name Hammer." The tree laughed, Milo laughed.

Milo hollered out "Thanks for everything!" and he raced away. Milo galloped at eighty miles an hour. The fairies, Raven, and Vulture flew above him.  They were all amazing, simply amazing!

All of a sudden, Milo put on his brakes; he came to a sliding stop! He thought, *White robe, gold trim, and purple sash, I wonder if I'll ever get to meet him, I wonder if he would like to ride me? I would love to put him to the test! Believe me, he better be the BEST of the BEST of the BEST or he will be lying in the dirt.* Milo bucked. His buck was lightning fast. Oh yes, that Milo Boy has really got spirit!

CHAPTER 37 | **A DIFFERENT KIND OF DIMENSION**

All of a sudden, Milo's nose hit an invisible wall! His nose smashed in, and his front teeth hit the barrier. Milo's sudden stop catapulted Raven and Vulture off of Milo's back. They hit the ground with a THUD! When they hit the ground, it jarred them pretty good. They stood up and staggered around.

Milo said, "Sorry about that, boys."

The fairies flew to the wall. They slowly flew along it; they were looking for a way past. The fairies flew back to Milo. "Milo, we think we have found a portal." They covered the portal with the *Blanket of Sparkling Mist*, and Milo stuck his head through the hole.

It was very bright! Milo had to wait for a bit to see. He squinted his eyes and let them adjust to the brightness. "Fairies, what do you think? Do we dare step in? It looks dangerous."

The landscape was very bleak—dirt, rocks, hills, ravines, no plant life.

Then a voice spoke out, "I dare you! I dare you to step in, Milo."

Milo stood motionless.

The voice spoke, "Chicken, chicken, chicken! Milo's a little chicken," and the voice laughed. "I double dare you, Milo, you little chicken! Milo's a scaredy cat. Milo's a wimp."

The voice started to get on Milo's nerves. Irritation filled his body.

"What are you afraid of, Milo? I heard you are supposed to be a great horse, but from what I can see, you are a coward."

Milo's muscles tightened, he began to frown. "Fairies, Vulture, Raven, what do you think? Should I go for it?"

"The decision is yours to make, Milo. Think about who you are, Milo, and what you represent."

Milo stood motionless. He calmed his nerves. Milo spoke, "Voice, are you sure you want me to step in, because I could end your existence."

"What? A little chicken like you could never end my existence!" and he laughed.

Milo began to smile, "Are you sure about that, Voice? Dare me one more time, Voice. You…little… chicken!"

Voice screamed out, "I DARE YOU, MILO!" and Voice laughed.

And Milo jumped through the portal. Milo lit on the bleak landscape. He stood on his hind legs and let out a huge whinny. The whinny rolled across the wasteland, it was so loud it hurt Voice's ears.

The voice thought, *Maybe I bit off more than I can chew.* And Voice hid behind a rock and peeked out at Milo. The voice thought, *Milo looks quite harmless.*

Milo hollered out, "Voice, you can't judge a book by its cover!"

*Now how did Milo know what I was thinking? I think I am in big trouble!* And Voice scampered away.

Milo walked to the top of a big hill. He looked over the land, nothing but rock and dry dirt.

Vulture and Raven flew off on a reconnaissance mission. They were gone for a long time. They came back and reported to Milo. "Milo, this could be the Land of Nothing. Milo, there is a large skeleton; it lies on the top of a hill. The hill is the highest point in this dimension. It is a full day's walk from here."

So Milo headed out. (It was great that Milo did not have to eat or drink, because there was no water in this dimension. You know, folks, no water…no food. Do you get it?) Milo continued on. He reached the top of the hill where the birds had seen the skeleton. It was gone!

"Milo, we are sure the skeleton was right here. I wonder what moved it?" They could see where it had been drug down the hill. "We will follow the trail."

The trail descended into a deep ravine. Milo made his way to the bottom. The bottom was a cool, dark place; there was just enough light so that they could barely see.

The fairies began to glow brightly, they lit up the area. The ground was covered with horse skeletons. The skeletons were laid out in perfect rows; they lay separately, none touching the others. The fairies counted them. There were 100 complete skeletons.

Milo was silent; he kept his calm, he showed no emotion. He walked up to the biggest skeleton and spoke, "Rise up and live again!" and he touched the skeleton with his nose.

The horse skeleton became whole again. The horse stood! He spoke, "It's been a long sleep, Milo. It is great to see you." Milo touched each skeleton. Soon there were 100 horses, whole again. They rose out of the canyon, they reached the top, and the wind began to blow. And as the wind blew across the land, the land became whole again.

Beautiful green grass, trees, flowers, and ponds appeared. It was done! It was Milo's second miracle.

The Voice appeared in front of Milo. The voice spoke, "Please forgive me, Milo?"

Milo reached out and touched Voice, "You are forgiven."

The voice began to sing, it was a beautiful song, and the voice drifted away on the wind.

Milo turned to the 100 horses. "Horses, this dimension is yours forever."

Milo and all the horses knelt, and the Top Being appeared, and he blessed them.

The 100 horses encircled Milo, and the leader said, "Milo, I will tell you the sad story of this dimension…Milo, this Dimension was exactly like the world. Its ecology was the same—water, animals, plants, trees, birds, fish, and humans. The humans classified themselves RICH, MIDDLE CLASS, POOR, and the ONE PERCENT."

Milo said, "I have heard the words 'One Percent' before. Justice mentioned them once."

"Yes, Milo, the One Percent controlled all the money in this dimension. The One Percent called the ninety-nine percent the Little People. They controlled the government. The government issued a weapons ban; they could not even have a knife with a sharp point!

"They controlled every aspect of the Little People's lives with their money—what they could eat, what they could drink. They built boxes around their heads and the Little People did not have the will to remove them."

Milo said, "I know a cowboy that lives in the world, and he took his box off and threw it away. And he has a horse and his name is Silent. And the cowboy and the horse will live and serve the Top Being forever, and happiness radiates from them."

"The One Percent exploited the land and the Little People. They piled their money in piles and constantly monitored each other's money piles—they would do anything to win the money pile contest!

"They controlled the Little People with lies, and the Little People believed their lies (because they would not remove the box that had been built around their heads). Television, news, government-knows-best, religion-knows-best, politicians-know-best, be passive, be nonviolent, be cowards, never question us….The Little People could not think for themselves.

"The Little People worked for the One Percent. They paid them just enough so they could afford a small house, and automobile, and for sure a television, the brain-washing machine. And the Little People watched television so much that they lost their ability to think. They turned into cowards and wimps.

"The One Percent gave the Little People drugs and alcohol, and it made them more passive yet. They cut their rate of pay. In order to keep their television, house, and automobile, the husband and wife both had to work; and this gave the One Percent the opportunity to completely control the Little People's children. And they made it possible for every child to have a computer phone—the ultimate, brainwashing machine!

"The One Percent pillaged the land. They dug and drilled for oil—they ruined the aquifer fields and cut down all the trees. And then they started to sell the water to the Little People that lived in the dry climates. They pumped the dimension dry. Everything started to die. Skeletons of animals lay across the landscape.

"Food became scarce, so the One Percent hired the Little People to collect the bones from all the dead. And they ground the bone into meal and sold the bone meal to the Little People for food. The Little People were hungry and thirsty. The One Percent rationed the bottled water to keep the 'bone pickers' alive as long as they could.

"Soon the bones were all gone, there was nothing left. The One Percent moved to a different dimension. No one knows for sure where they went. Could they have moved into the world? Seems likely. Everyone and everything was dead. Everything turned to dust, and the wind blew the dust away."

Milo thought it seemed like the world was headed down the same path. And it was very possible that he was the only one that could change the world's destiny.

Milo walked off. He walked across the new land and he left his hoof prints on the land. And every hoof print turned into a tree, a flower, an animal. It was the BEST of the BEST of the BEST! Milo would find a portal; his journey would continue.

(Well, folks, I bet you are wondering who or what drug the horse skeleton down the hill and into the deep canyon? Could it have been the human dressed in the white robe with gold trim and a purple sash? Or could it be a special force that Milo knows nothing about? Time will tell.)

## CHAPTER 38 | **THE SCORPION**

Milo was exhausted from the day's events. He lay down on the top of a huge hill and he looked out over the new land. His brothers sat next to him. Milo spoke. "I must sleep."

The fairies began to hum and Milo's mind drifted off into his wonderful dream world. The fairies, Vulture, and Raven looked at each other, Vulture spoke. "My brothers, let's surprise Milo. Let's take Milo back to his dimension while he sleeps." The fairies cast a spell over Milo; they picked Milo up and flew him back to his dimension.

They entered Milo's dimension from above, it was the first time they had ever did this. They were right above Mirror Lake.

The fairies set Milo's sleeping body under the apple tree, and Milo slept till morning. When Milo awoke, he did not open his eyes. He sniffed the air, the scent of apples entered his nostrils, his eyes popped open, and he jumped to his feet. He could not believe where he was. Milo let out a huge whinny, and the sound of Milo's whinny rolled across Mirror Lake.

The fairies flew to Milo, they tickled Milo and he began to laugh. Milo's laugh was beautiful, and then Milo began to sing a horse song. When the song was finished, Milo reached up, picked an apple, and ate it.

The fairies, Vulture, and Raven gathered around Milo. Vulture spoke. "Well what's next?"

"I will travel alone to the desert."

"Milo, do you think it will be safe to travel alone?"

"Vulture, I will be fine. You know Vulture, I have been blessed with reflexes like the speed of lightning. I am very confident in myself, and Vulture, I will be very careful."

"Milo, it is good to have confidence, it is good to feel good about oneself; but, do not forget to add humility to this feeling. Milo, I have flown over the desert many times in search of food. Milo, there is a huge Scorpion that lives in the desert, be aware of this at all times."

"Thanks for warning me Vulture. Brothers, meet me in the desert in two weeks or fourteen days! Either way is fine." Everyone laughed! Milo trotted off.

Milo soon found a portal, sand spewed from it. He walked slowly through the portal and kept his eyes closed. He felt the hot sand on his hooves, he opened his eyes very slowly, he kept his eyes half closed and the sand swirled around him.

Milo looked across the desert landscape. *What a wasteland.*

Milo smelled the air. There was a faint smell of evil in the air. Milo's panoramic vision was a real gift. He could see completely around himself. His ears listened intensely for the slightest sound, the smell of evil intensified! Milo's ears picked up on a strange sound. Off in the distance a funnel cloud appeared. The funnel cloud of sand was coming right toward Milo at a terrific speed. Milo's muscles tightened, the smell of evil intensified to a point that almost burned his nose. Milo sneezed! The funnel cloud of sand was 300 yards from Milo. From out of the cloud stepped a huge scorpion. Its huge stinger was whipping the air, making a snapping sound. The scorpion raced towards Milo. Milo was amazed at the scorpion's speed! The scorpion tried to sting Milo several times, but Milo was too fast for him. The scorpion stopped his attack, he hissed at Milo; his breath was so stinky it almost made Milo puke.

The scorpion spoke. "Milo Boy, what are you doing here?"

"Scorpion, I have come here to pray."

"And who do you pray for, Milo Boy?"

"Scorpion, I pray for you and evil."

The Scorpion hissed and began to laugh. His laugh was a wicked laugh; it made Milo shiver.

"Milo, why would you pray for me?"

"I pray for you because your destiny is the Land of Nothing!"

"How do you know this Milo?"

"The Top Being told me this."

"And who is the Top Being?"

"The Top Being is the creator, he even created you!"

The Scorpion hissed and scowled. "Milo, I have an offer for you. I can make you all-powerful, you will be able to control the Little People in the world, you will be a member of the One Percent. Not even the Top Being will be able to control you; you will have to answer to no one. I will grant you this Milo; all you have to do is let me sting you!"

Milo hollered out, "Be gone Scorpion!"

The Scorpion hissed. "Milo, you are a fool." The Scorpion tried to sting Milo, but the Scorpion missed and he stung himself! The stinger sunk deep into his body, he screamed a blood-curdling scream, his body began to smoke and wither.

He spoke in his hissing way, "Milo I will return someday, and vengeance will be mine!" The Scorpion's body turned to dust; Wind came and blew his dust away.

Wind blew on Milo, his mane and tail fluttered in the wind, the air around Milo began to sparkle.

Milo began to chant.

His chanting gave honor to the Top Being, the Holy Cow, and the human dressed in white, trimmed in gold and with a purple sash.

Milo prayed that the people in the world would become grateful people, for gratefulness and appreciation will make your soul shine with a heavenly light.

The days passed, and soon it was the fourteenth day. The fairies, Vulture and Raven came flying in.

Vulture spoke. "Milo, did you run into the Scorpion?"

"Oh yes, Vulture."

"Well Milo, how did the meeting go?"

"Well Vulture, let me put it this way. I really smoked him."

Vulture and Raven laughed. Milo laughed, the fairies looked puzzled. Sometimes the fairies could be kind of clueless.

Well folks, that Scorpion sure was one bad character. Do you remember what he said before he turned to dust?

"Milo, I will return someday, and vengeance will be mine." How is this possible? Could it be the Scorpion has a spirit hiss?

CHAPTER 39 | **THE LOST CHILDREN**

Vulture, Raven, and the fairies escorted Milo out of the desert and back into his dimension.

Milo laid down and the *Blanket of Sparkling Mist* hovered over him.

Milo dreamt about Inferno and Justice and George.

As Frog would say: brothers, brothers, brothers.

Milo awoke and to his surprise there stood Inferno and Justice and George.

"George, we will go to British Columbia. We will be searching for some lost children."

"How do you know this, Milo?"

"George, the Holy Cow can predict the future. She said we must find a portal into the world. She told me that we do not have much time, so we will leave immediately."

The fairies flew from Milo's mane. They would look for a portal. Raven and Vulture flew out on a reconnaissance mission. Milo's dimension was a fantastic place! There were deserts, mountains, rolling plains, and, yes, there was Mirror Lake—Milo's Lake—and Milo's apple tree. And, yes, there are the huge trees that Rabbit takes care of.

Milo began to sing, and Inferno joined in, and then George and Justice broke into song. Milo's heart was full of joy. He loved his brothers and he knew his brothers loved him; and now, he was trying to rescue a family.

Milo and everyone traveled all day and all night. There was still no sign of a portal. They were not apprehensive though; their faith in the Holy Cow was unshakable. They knew there would be a portal; it was just a matter of time! Never did they lose faith in the Holy Cow. As Frog would say, "Never, never, never lose faith."

The team continued on into the second day. They came to a river, the water flowed swiftly along, and they stopped and talked things over. All of a sudden, a beautiful brook trout jumped out of the water. The brook trout hollered out, "Hey, you guys follow me!" and she headed upstream. They came to a huge whirlpool. Milo watched the water spin around. It made him dizzy.

The trout swam over to everyone. The trout spoke, "The whirlpool is a portal. Jump in."

And then the Holy Cow's face appeared in the water. She was beautiful! The Holy Cow looked into everyone's eyes, and a feeling of love and trust entered their bodies. There was nothing they would not do for her.

Milo jumped into the whirlpool and everyone followed. They entered into the world. Milo and everyone were soaking wet! The horses all shook, and the water sprayed from their bodies. George placed his sword; tip first, in the ground. He stood close to his sun-sword—he soon would be dry.

They were in a beautiful mountain forest. It was British Columbia! They would now start looking for the lost children. The team spread out and began to slowly walk through the forest. They jumped up many wild animals as they walked along. They broke out of the forest into a large, cut-over area. There was a hillside ahead, it was blue in color, they walked to the hillside and began to climb the slope. The ground was covered with blueberries.

Milo picked the berries and tasted them, "Hey, gang, try the berries. They are The Best of the Best of the Best!"

Everyone loved the blueberries.

Milo, Justice, and Inferno sniffed the air, "What is that smell?"

Milo said, "I have smelled that before. It is the smell of evil!" Everyone stood silently.

Raven and Vulture took to the air—their keen eyes scanned the landscape. Then they spotted a huge bear!

The bear was eating blueberries about one-half mile away. They flew back to Milo and Inferno and George and Justice and reported their findings.

Inferno said, "If there is a bear in this area, we must move out. It is not safe here."

So everyone climbed to the top of the hill and descended the other side. When they reached the base of the hill, there was a small trout stream. It was a beautiful sight! The water bubbled and sparkled as it ran along.

Milo laughed at the little trout that were swimming in the stream.

All of a sudden, the word "bear" entered Milo's mind. *What was Inferno talking about?*

"Inferno, what is a bear?"

"Oh, Milo, the bear is a magnificent animal. The Top Being pulled out all the stops when He created the bear. He made many kinds of bears because he loved them so much. Many of their actions are human-like. He gave them the keenest nose on the planet earth. He made their disposition unpredictable—one minute they act like a pet, the next instant they will tear you to pieces.

"He made them look so friendly that the humans make little stuffed bears—they call them Teddy Bears. The Top Being did this because he loves to mess with humans' minds. He loves to test humans' intelligence. The Top Being laughs at them; He cries for them, he loves them with an unconditional love. And he hopes they love him in the same way."

Everyone shouted at the same time, "AMEN!"

The "AMEN!" echoed through the incredible forest of British Columbia. The word "AMEN!" was heard by the five lost children; they had wandered away from the family's campsite.

A small rabbit had run through their campsite, and the children had chased after it. Mother and Father had stayed at the camp; they did not realize that the children would stray so far away. The children stopped the chase.

The oldest boy said, "We better get back to camp," He reached in his pocket to check his compass. It was not there! He had changed his pants that morning and had forgotten his compass. A feeling of panic entered his body. *I must be calm so I do not scare the children.*

He began to pray, "Dear God, give me the strength to overcome my panic. Let me be a leader. Help me save my brothers and sisters." A feeling of strength entered his body. Could this boy's God be the same as Milo's Top Being? (For nothing is impossible for the Top Being, and nothing is impossible for the boy's God.)

The boy and his brothers and sisters held hands and began to pray. As they prayed in silence, they heard the word "AMEN!" echoing through the forest.

The children hollered back, "AMEN!"

The three horse's ears stood straight up, they hollered out, "AMEN!"

And the children answered with an, "AMEN!"

Raven and Vulture said, "Keep up the conversation, and we will fly and find out who it is."

So Milo, Inferno, George, and Justice continued to communicate, and the children answered back.

It wasn't long, and Raven and Vulture found the five children. Vulture circled the sky above the children, and Raven flew back to Milo. It wouldn't be long, and Milo and the children would be united!

Soon Milo could smell the children, "We are getting really close."

George spoke, "Justice, chant the words 'Amen, Amen, Amen.'"

So Justice did this, his voice was beautiful.

The children sang back to Justice, his chanting calmed them, and serenity overtook them. They were found!

George walked up to the children, the children encircled him. He said, "Children, do not be afraid," and Milo, Inferno, and Justice walked up.

George said, "Children, you are going to experience a very wonderful thing. These horses are going to talk to you."

Milo stepped forward and spoke, "Children, you will be safe with us, for we are the most gifted horses to ever walk on the face of the earth." Milo, Justice, and Inferno gave them a bow.

Inferno introduced himself—the children were amazed at his size and his beauty.

Then Justice stepped forward. Justice began to chant, "Oh, my dear children, how special you are! I christen you 'Knights of the Forest,' created by my Top Being and your God. Your lives will be sacred forever. Amen."

The air began to sparkle around the children. The fairies flew from Milo's mane. The children were amazed the way the fairies flew through the sparkling air.

Raven and Vulture flew in; they landed in front of the children.

Raven spoke, "Welcome to Milo's world."

Vulture spread his wings and hopped toward the children. The children jumped backwards.

Vulture spoke, "Just testing your reflexes," and Vulture laughed. Vulture could be a bit unpredictable.

George spoke, "Children, we will stay here for the night. Be confident in us. There is nothing in the world or the Universe that can hurt you."

Darkness slowly crept into the forest.

Milo and Justice lay down and the children sat and leaned against them. The *Blanket of Sparkling Mist* hovered over them. Inferno stood guard. Raven and Vulture slept in the trees. The forest echoed with the howling of timber wolves, the yipping of coyotes, and the hooting of owls.

George placed his sword, tip first, into the ground. It emitted a soft light, and the warmth from the sword kept them warm. Milo, Justice, and the children slept.

The Top Being and the children's God looked down on them. They nodded to each other and they sprinkled their Blessed Dust on them. It was done!

The children slept soundly all night. They awoke as the sun's rays came streaking through the trees.

Milo and Justice stood. They stretched and yawned. The events of the day would begin....

The children told Milo about the big river that they and their parents were camped by.

Raven and Vulture flew off to search for the river. They soon returned and flew in, "Milo, there is a huge bear only one-quarter mile ahead! He is headed this way!"

The bear was a massive grizzly bear. He could smell the horses and the children. He began to lick his lips. *Breakfast straight ahead!*

Milo, Inferno, Justice, and George stood motionless—the children huddled behind them.  George spoke, "If I have to withdraw my sword, everyone, close your eyes—for the sun-sword will blind you."

Inferno stepped forward, "Never mind, George. This bear is mine." The purple haze began to swirl around Inferno, his muscles tightened, his eyes began to glow.

The huge bear charged Inferno. His teeth snapped together, saliva poured from his mouth. Inferno charged the bear; he took him head-on as a cavalry horse would. When Inferno and the bear collided, it sounded like thunder. The force of the collision knocked the bear out. Inferno stood over the bear and pawed the ground. The dirt flew from his hooves.

Milo walked up to Inferno. "Is he dead?"

"No, Milo, I did not take his life." Inferno bit five claws off the bear—two from one paw and one from the other three. The bear slowly regained consciousness. The bear stood, he shook his huge body. He gave Inferno a bow and turned and walked away.

Inferno walked over to the children and gave each one of them a bear claw. The claws were long and sharp. Inferno began to laugh and everyone joined in. What a wonderful horse he was! He could have killed the bear with ease, but he let him live.

The Top Being looked down from above and smiled. He thought, *Oh, Inferno, I am so proud of you— you have never let me down—how merciful you are!*

Raven and Vulture flew off to find the children's parents. It wasn't long. They spotted the search party and the parents. They flew back to Milo. "Milo, follow us." They led Milo to the children's parents.

Milo, George, and Justice stood behind the trees so the parents and the search party could not see them. The parents hugged them and began to cry. The whole family looked up and thanked their God.

A vulture and a raven flew above them. The children waved at Vulture and Raven. They hollered out, "Goodbye!"

Their parents got a puzzled look on their faces. The children told them about Milo, George, Justice, and Inferno—about the fairies, about Raven and Vulture. The parents thought that the children were traumatized by their experience. They gave each child a hug. They looked at each other with love in their eyes.

The youngest boy said, "Mom, Dad, look what Inferno gave us." He pulled the huge, bear claw from out of his pocket—the blood on the end was still fresh. And the other four children stepped forward and showed them their bear claws.

It was done.

## CHAPTER 40 | **DULUTH AND LAKE SUPERIOR**

Milo stood atop Spirit Mountain. He looked out over a huge glacier; it covered the land as far as his eyes could see. The Spirit Winds swirled around him, his mane and tail fluttering in the breeze. He was a sight to behold!

The fairies flew around him; their colors seemed to sparkle in the wind.  Raven and Vulture circled on high.  The sun glistened off the vast ice field. It was truly a majestic sight! The sun's heat intensified, the ice began to melt. The ice field slowly turned to water—beautiful, clear, clean water. Yes, the gift of life!  A mighty lake began to form. Milo stood motionless, only his mane and tail moved in the wind.

Wind began to speak, "Milo, you are watching the formation of the five Great Lakes. The lake you are looking at will be called Lake Superior."

As the ice melted, the body of water grew larger and larger, and now there was water as far as Milo's eyes could see. The water began to move in the wind. It continuously changed in color as it moved. The waves got bigger and the tops broke into a white mist.

Wind spoke, "Milo, I call those waves 'white caps.'"

Milo still did not move. His eyes slowly focused to the right side and a small body of water formed.

Wind spoke, "Milo, that small body of water is called a bay. The ice that was on the land began to melt, the water ran toward the lower points of land, and it ran toward the bay."

Wind spoke again, "Milo, that water that runs toward the bay will be called a river."

Wind said, "Milo, the landmass on your left will be called the North Shore, and the landmass on your right will be called the South Shore. And rivers will flow from these landmasses and flow into the lake."

Milo thought, *My right. My left. What does Wind mean?*

The fairies flew to Milo, they gathered on his left. They touched Milo's left shoulder, "Milo, this is your left." Then they flew to Milo's right shoulder and touched Milo's right shoulder. "Milo, this is your right."

Milo paused. Milo thought, *Right…left…Cool! Fairies…north…south.* He laughed, "What does Wind mean?"

"Milo, it is called direction. The earth has a North Pole and a South Pole. Right now, north is on your left, south is on your right. You are looking toward the sun as it rises from the lake that is east. Your tail is pointing west."

Milo laughed, "You mean the sun comes out of the lake?"

"No, Milo, the sun is in the sky."

"The sky?"

"Yes, Milo, the blueness above you."

"You said it rises from the lake."

The fairies said, "Oh, Milo, Milo, Milo, we better change the subject."

Milo laughed. "I sure do get confused at times. Right…left…North Pole…South Pole…north…south… east…west…direction…sun rises from the water…sun rises in the sky…sun rises in the east. Wow! I wonder who thought all this up! Hey, Fairies, when the sun rises from the water and then it travels in the sky, where does it travel to?"

"Milo, it heads west."

"Oh, where my butt is pointed?"

"Yes, Milo."

"What does it do then?"

"Milo, the sun sets."

"Well, where does it sit?"

"It doesn't."

"Well, you just said it did."

"The sun goes down."

"Well, where does it go down to?"

"Milo, forget it. Change the subject."

Milo thought, *Sometimes I think, as Chassie would say, "Those fairies are all nuts, they have totally lost their marbles!"* Milo laughed. He reared up and let out a huge whinny, its sound rolled across Lake Superior. It was the first whinny the lake had ever heard.

Milo turned his attention back to the lake, and the lake and the land began to evolve. It was like watching the lake and the land moving through time.

A boat appeared on the lake. Smoke from campfires onshore curled into the air. The humans had arrived with more boats—sailboats, canoes, steamboats. The boats got bigger and bigger. Buildings sprang up on both sides of the lake and the bay. The cities of Duluth and Superior were on the move, bigger and bigger they grew. The time flew by. Bridges were built. Railroads were built. All of a sudden, a huge storm formed over the lake. The sky turned coal black. Huge lightning bolts blasted through the clouds and the sky. Milo braced himself against the wind and the storm. The rains drenched Milo. He stood motionless. The storm stopped. The sun peeked out. Wind said, "Come on out, Sun!" and the sun appeared in all its glory.

Milo shook his rain-soaked body. The sun felt good as it warmed him. It was the year 2018. The two cities had been completely formed.

The fairies flew from Milo's mane. Vulture and Raven flew from the oak trees where they had weathered the storm. Raven lit on Milo's back, "Tonight, we will walk through the city of Duluth."

The sun went down. Milo looked behind himself; he was looking over his butt. He chuckled.*Those fairies never did tell me where the sun goes to! I bet they don't know.* Milo turned his head back to the lake. It was dark out, the lights from the cities of Duluth and Superior sparkled in the darkness. The bridges were beautiful. The old lift bridge was lit up, Milo marveled at its structure.

The moon rose in the night sky, its light reflected off the water. The fairies spoke, "Well, Milo, let's venture into the city." They walked down Spirit Mountain. They walked through the neighborhoods. Milo stepped onto Grand Avenue, and his feet "clopped" as his hooves hit the pavement.

The fairies spoke, "Milo, we will walk the center line of the street. Do not be afraid, Milo, the automobiles will not hit you. We have control of them."

The humans in their automobiles whizzed by, they were going nowhere fast.

Milo walked up the on-ramp and stepped onto the freeway, the cars went flying by. Milo walked the median between the northbound and southbound lanes. The cars were going nowhere, faster than ever!

Milo spoke, "Fairies, how fast are the automobiles going?"

"Oh, 60 miles per hour, Milo."

"Is that as fast as their cars will go?"

"Oh, no, Milo, those cars could travel as fast as 100 to 150 miles per hour. The speed limit is 55 miles per hour here."

"So the humans have a speed limit they must travel at?"

"Oh, yes, Milo, otherwise they would all travel as fast as their cars would go. Most humans have no common sense; when they get into their cars, they go nuts!"

*Go nuts...no marbles....* Milo laughed, "Strange species, I would say!" Milo stepped off the freeway. He walked into the area called Canal Park.

## CHAPTER 41 | **EXPLORING DULUTH**

Milo could smell horse poop. Lo and behold, there were the horses and buggies! Milo was surprised to see the horses.

The horses all spoke at once, "Hi, Milo, great to see you!" Milo wondered if there were any horses that Chassie didn't know.

The horses told Milo how they loved to pull the buggies around. "Milo, it is so good to be useful."

"We love the people, and they love us."

"We know this because we can read their minds."

"We make the children happy. Many children have never seen a horse up close and touched them. We wish we could talk to them, but that is not possible because the Top Being made us this way. Many people think we should not be here, but they do not understand! Our purpose in life is not to eat in a pasture and never be useful. Our purpose is to serve mankind, and we love doing it!"

"We love to compete. We love to pull. We love to race, and we love to be admired for our looks and our grace. For horses we are, we are the best by far. Yes, horses, we are!"

Milo said, "Yes, as Frog would say, 'Horses are the BEST of the BEST of the BEST,' and we all have four legs!" Milo did a little jig, and every horse hollered out, "Hip-Hip-Hooray!"

Milo was so happy! He loved talking to the horses. His ears perked up, he could hear horses coming—their feet clopped as they walked along. Milo turned and looked up the street, and two horses walked toward Milo. Their riders were dressed in uniforms. The riders and the horses looked very stately. The riders were police officers.

The horses spoke, "Hello, horse, great to see you. I see you are alone."

Milo spoke, "Oh, no, I am not alone. Look up."

The police horses looked up. A vulture and a raven flew above. The police horses laughed. "Those birds are your friends?"

Milo spoke, "No, they are my brothers."

Raven and Vulture swooped down and lit next to Milo.

The police horses spoke, "It is a pleasure to meet you all. Welcome to Duluth!"

Milo touched both horses with his nose, and brotherhood entered their bodies.

The police horses both spoke at once. "Holy Cow, you are Milo! We were wondering if we would ever get to meet you!"

Milo took a bow.

"Well, Milo, we must move on." And the police officers turned their horses and they walked away.

(All the time Milo was talking to the police horses, the Top Being had frozen the police officers' minds in time. They did not know that the horse's conversation had taken place. It would be great, if someday, humans and horses could speak to each other. Maybe, if we all wish hard enough, the Top Being would let this happen.)

Milo walked to the canal between the lake and the bay. A ship was just entering the canal.

Milo spoke, "Fairies that is one big ship!"

"Yes, Milo, it came from the ocean."

Milo spoke, "Is the ocean close to here?"

"Oh, no, Milo, it is 2,038 nautical miles or 2,342 miles away. It takes eight and a half days of sailing to get here."

Milo walked along the shore of the lake. The rocky shore was strange for Milo to walk on. The fairies flew ahead of Milo, they were looking for agates. They found one and brought it to Milo. Milo was amazed at its beauty. The fairies polished it, and it became more beautiful. Then they split it in

two, its colors were amazing!

Milo spoke, "Who made this stone?"

"The Top Being made this stone when time began." The fairies put the stone together and put it back in its place.

Milo loved his lesson on agates. It was easy for him to understand.

They approached a huge building. It was beautiful. "That is a house, Milo. Humans lived there and so did horses."

"Horses lived there?"

"Yes, Milo, we will show you their home. Milo, the horses lived in here." They opened the door to the stables. It was beautiful inside. The stalls had cork on the floors.

Milo stepped in, the cork felt good on his feet.

The fairies spoke, "The humans took excellent care of their horses. The horses were their only means of transportation; they pulled their sleighs and buggies."

Milo thought, "They couldn't have made it without us!"

The fairies said, "Milo, this is the Glensheen Mansion." They showed Milo around. He could not believe how beautiful it was. "Well, Milo, it is time to move out."

Milo stepped into the Glensheen Garden, the vegetables smelled wonderful. Just then, two F-16s from the Duluth Air Guard flew overhead. The roar from the engines hurt Milo's ears.

"Milo, those are fighter jets."

"What are they for?"

"They are used for war and defense."

Milo became very serious, "War, I know all about war. Inferno taught me everything about war."

The Fairies spoke, "Milo, we are going to take you to the air force base."

So Milo walked up the big hill from the lake to the high ground. Milo could see the lights from the airport. He walked towards them, and there it was—the entrance to the air base.

The fairies said, "Milo, we will enter into the air base. We will make you invisible."

So Milo walked up to the fence with ease. He jumped the fence. When Milo's feet hit the ground, they made a thumping sound. The guards looked around, but there was nothing in sight. Milo walked up to them and touched them with his nose, and the guards jumped back from the touch.

They sounded the alarm, and the air base snapped to attention. Everyone ran around like they were nuts. The pilots ran to their F-16s and took off. The sound was deafening. The fairies plugged Milo's ears, so his hearing would not be damaged. Milo thought, *I have never gotten a reaction like that before just from a nose touch!* and he laughed. Everyone was running around looking for something that could not be seen.

Milo said, "Being invisible is really fun!" Milo trotted to the runway. When he stepped onto the runway, he did a tap dance on the pavement. Raven and Vulture were flying above; they were watching the chaos below. They laughed so hard, they almost collided in mid-air.

The F-16s were flying in formation. The fairies took over the controls—the pilots were helpless. The fairies flew the planes to 30,000 feet. The vapor trails were visible in the beautiful blue sky. They kept the planes in a tight formation and wrote Milo's name in the sky. Everyone for miles in all directions could read Milo's name. The vapor trail name would drift across the United States. The fairies gave the controls back to the pilots. They could not believe what had happened to them, but they kept calm through the whole ordeal.

(You see, these pilots were the BEST of the BEST of the BEST. You see, they were the Duluth Air Guard Pilots, part of the United States Air Force—the greatest air force in the world!)

What happened that day at the Duluth Air Base was instantly classified. The news media reported about the name "Milo" that was written in the sky. Pictures made it on national television. Some people recognized the name "Milo" (the people at the Kentucky Derby that had heard the name "Milo" did, and the people at the Suicide Race in Omak, Washington…but no one else).  But the pilots were ordered not to speak about it, and the events of that day soon would be forgotten.

All the animals recognized the name "Milo" though—all the birds, every living thing, fish, insects, trees, flowers, timber wolves (for sure). And then there were the horses—every horse in the United States bowed their heads and said a prayer for Milo.

It was done.

## CHAPTER 42 | **ISLE ROYALE**

Milo, the fairies, Raven, and Vulture headed up the North Shore of Lake Superior. They told Milo that he would witness one of the great wonders of the world, the North Shore of Lake Superior. The rivers, the waterfalls, the cliffs, and the trees.

Milo drank the water from the lake. It was not as good as the water in Mirror Lake, but it was quite good. The huge lake was awesome; it had a special smell, it had a special color. The mighty lake had done well at fighting off pollution. The water was very cold.

Milo walked into the water. It was cold on his legs, but it felt good.  The wind began to blow and soon the waves came. They got bigger. And then the Lake spoke.

Milo jumped out of the water. The mighty Lake scared Milo. Its voice was like thunder, "Hello, horse, and how are you today?"

Milo looked startled. He did not answer.

"Horse, I asked you a question. Please answer me."

Milo stuttered, "I…am…am…f.f.fine."

The Lake splashed its cold water on Milo. It was so cold; it took Milo's breath away.

He was soaked. He shook. The water flew from Milo's body in a fine mist.

The fairies flew from Milo's mane. They were drenched. They began to glow brightly. They instantly dried.

The mighty Lake laughed, "Milo, I may seem cruel, but you must accept me, for you have no other choice.  You must respect me, for you have no other choice. Milo, I make my own weather. I make my own storms. You see, Milo, no one has control over me. The Top Being made me this way!"

And he laughed, his laugh was deafening. "Milo, I can sink the mighty ships that the humans build. I can break them in two. You see, Milo, the ocean and I have no mercy. If you do not respect us, we will swallow you up. Your end will come!" And he laughed again.

"Yes, Milo, the ocean and I were created to humble the egotistical humans. We are the mightiest of Mother Nature. You might think I am cruel, but this is how the Top Being keeps the humans in check. The humans try to pollute us; their greed for money overwhelms their common sense. But we will prevail, for Mother Nature has sworn an oath to the Top Being. If she has to, she will drive humans into extinction."

Milo said, "I have thought about that myself. For, Lake, my brother Inferno and I could accomplish the same feat. Yes, Lake, we could end their existence." And Milo laughed—his laugh was not a laugh of joy— it was a laugh of determination, a laugh of commitment. It was a laugh the fairies had never heard before, and it made them shiver.…

The Lake spoke, "Milo, I want you to go to Isle Royale," and the lake became calm—it became smooth as glass. The sunlight glowed off the lake, it was almost blinding.

Milo touched his nose to the Lake, his reflection was awesome. Milo stepped into the lake. The water was not as cold as before. The lake had changed its temperature so Milo could swim to Isle Royale safely.

Milo entered the water. He began to swim. The scenery was beautiful! Milo's head and neck and the top of his back were above the water. A wake extended out from his body.

A seagull flew in and lit on Milo's back. "Hello, horse, great day for a swim."

Milo said, "How did you know that I am a horse ?"

"Milo, I spend a lot of time in Duluth and Superior. There are horses at Canal Park."

"Yes, bird, I know all of them. They are my brothers."

"Yes," the seagull said, "brotherhood is wonderful, Milo. We seagulls are all brothers."

Milo spoke, "Yes, Seagull, if only humans were all brothers, there would be peace in the world."

The seagull looked into the water. "Hey, horse, there is a lake trout headed our way."

A huge lake trout came swimming up from the depths. It surfaced alongside of Milo. "Hi, horse, headed for Isle Royale?"

"Yes, fish! It is great to see you."

"So, horse, you know I am a fish?"

"Oh yes, I have swum in the Columbia River. I met a salmon, a sturgeon, and a walleye while I swam there. They were great to talk to. I swam underwater with them, it was quite an experience!"

"Hey, horse, how fast can you swim?"

"I really don't know."

"Well, horse, you have to get your body to plane out. Speed up and your body will rise out of the water, and it will not plow along."

So Milo began to gallop. His body slowly began to rise out of the water. Milo began to gallop faster and faster. Soon his whole body was out of the water. His speed increased, and then he turned it on! Milo began to gallop on top of the water, only his hooves were touching the water. He was surprised! The water seemed hard. It gave him great traction. He was running ON TOP of the water! He couldn't believe his speed was 95 miles per hour! He had left the seagull and the lake trout far behind. Isle Royale loomed ahead. It was beautiful!

Milo slowed. His body slowly sank into the water. He resumed his regular swimming speed. The seagull and lake trout caught up.

"Horse, that was nuts what you just did!"

"Yes," Milo said, "I can run faster than the wind can blow, and now I know that my gift also works on water. Thank you, Holy Cow!"

Raven and Vulture watched from above. They were amazed! The fairies had flown with them (they did not want to ride Milo at that speed in case he hit a rock and sank. They had forgotten about Milo's gift that he would live forever. They really had nothing to fear. The fairies had just lost faith for a short time. Sometimes, that happens to all of us).

Milo swam into a beautiful bay. It almost took Milo's breath away.

"Fairies, can you believe this?" And then a huge cow moose raised her head out of the water. Milo had not noticed her at first. He jumped! "Fairies, what is that?"

"It's a moose, Milo."

Milo walked toward the moose. Milo had not noticed her calf that was walking with her. "Is that her child?"

"Yes, Milo, that is a cow moose and her calf."

Milo spoke, "As in Holy Cow?"

"Yes, Milo, a mother moose is called a cow; her child is called a calf." The moose walked up to Milo. Milo stood motionless. The cow touched Milo with her nose—the touch rippled through Milo's body.

Milo spoke, "Fairies, she is sacred like Justice and Eagle."

Milo bowed his head. The cow moose filled her mouth with water.

She held the water in her huge mouth. She swung her head above Milo's, and let the water out of her mouth. The water fell on Milo's head—he was baptized!

She spoke, "Milo, you will spread brotherhood throughout the world, and peace will prevail. Milo, as Frog would say, 'Amen, Amen, Amen.' "

*How does she know Frog? Maybe Frog is very special and I did not realize it!* Milo's heart had a feeling of joy in it.

The fairies, Raven, and Vulture watched this special time in Milo's life from above, with tears in their eyes. Can you believe it? Vulture actually cried. It was the second time he had experienced this emotion. It was the BEST of the BEST of the BEST! The cow and the calf walked out of the water. Milo followed behind. Their wake rippled across the bay. They stepped onto the shore.

The calf said, "Milo, I want you to meet my father."

They walked into the woods. The calf said, "There he is!"

Milo looked around. He could see nothing. Milo said, "I do not see him."

"Look up, Milo."

Milo looked up and, above the brush tops, a huge set of antlers appeared. They were MASSIVE!

The calf said, "Do not be afraid, Milo, for Mother and I are with you. If we were not with you, you would want to avoid him."

They walked up to the huge bull; he was much larger than Milo. "Hello horse," his voice rumbled like a bass drum. "I heard you were coming to Isle Royale…Hey, horse, I overheard some timber wolves talking about you. The word has spread through a lot of wolf packs about your 'apostle wolves.' A lot of wolves now kill deer with a quick bite to the neck."

The huge bull moose turned and walked away. Milo said his goodbyes to the cow and the calf and walked out of the forest. Milo thought about the huge bull moose. He was not friendly. He did not touch him, and Milo could sense he did not want to be touched. He was very special. The Top Being had made him that way, and Milo was not about to question either of them about it.

Milo walked back to the shoreline. He stepped into the water. He would swim back to the North Shore. Milo did not run on top of the water. He swam along, and all the fish in Lake Superior and all the birds traveled with him. And they sang a wonderful song; it was a song of joy and a song of peace.

Milo reached the shoreline. The fairies said, "Milo, it is time to look for a portal." Milo and the fairies came to the border between the United States and Canada. They walked up to the border patrol agents. Both the United States agents and Canadian agents looked at Milo in amazement.

The fairies said, "Well, lookie here, a portal between the two countries." Both border patrol agents walked toward Milo. The fairies stretched the *Blanket of Sparkling Mist* across the portal, and Milo disappeared. He had entered a different dimension. The border patrol agents walked around, looking for the horse that had disappeared. They talked to each other and agreed not to mention anything about the incident. If they did, they would lose their jobs and would have to submit to psychiatric exams.

Vulture and Raven watched the agents. They swooped down, flew over the agents' heads, and flew through the portal.

It was done.

## CHAPTER 43 | **THE LAND OF WRITERS AND ARTISTS**

It was dark in the dimension that Milo had entered. The fairies glowed brightly. Raven and Vulture sat on Milo's back.

Milo said, "We will wait here until the light comes." Milo stood for over an hour in the dark.

The fairies said, "I hope it gets light soon."

And then a ray of light streaked across the sky. It was beautiful! And then, the sky became full of streaks of light, they were every color you could imagine!

Milo said, "Fairies, where are we?"

"Milo, we are in the Land of Writers and Artists."

Everything that Milo looked at was a painting. Everything the Top Being had created in this dimension was a painting—the sky, the ground Milo walked on, the forest, the plains, the mountains, the "everything," and the "nothing" was a painting.

The humans,

the animals,

the birds,

the horses,

the frogs,

the turtles—EVERYTHING WAS A PAINTING!

It was strange for Milo, he was puzzled. *Am I a painting? Are Vulture, Raven and the fairies paintings?* He looked at them. They looked real.

Milo rubbed his head with his hoof. "Man, this is real confusing. Fairies, can you explain this to me?"

"Yes, Milo. We all came from a human's mind. The Top Being put us in the human's mind. He wrote what was in his mind. And then, an Artist created our image, and we became real. We are real, Milo! Everything that we deal with is real!"

Milo said, "This is driving me nuts. I must stop thinking about it!" Milo walked along. There was a huge hill ahead, he climbed the hill. When he was just about to the top, he looked out over a beautiful valley, it was dotted with flowers.

There was another hill in the distance. Milo could see a human sitting on the top of the hill; he was sitting on a rock. The human was writing a book.

Milo thought, *That is strange.*

Milo reached the top of the hill he was climbing. To his surprise, there was a human sitting there painting a picture. The human was a woman; she had her back to Milo. She was painting a picture of a woman that was painting a picture of a woman. A horse was standing behind her—the horse was Milo! The Writer stopped writing, and the Artist stopped painting. Milo tried to move; he was frozen in time. The Writer began to write, and the woman began to paint, and Milo began to move. The Writer wrote about a horse galloping. The artist painted a horse that was galloping. Milo started galloping. The . Writer kept writing. The artist painted a raven, a vulture, and fairies traveling with Milo.

She painted a horse, a raven, a vulture, and fairies jumping through a portal—a *Blanket of Sparkling Mist* in front of them!

Milo's hooves hit the ground; they were in the dimension that Milo was born in. Milo came to a sliding stop.

Raven, the fairies, and Vulture touched each other and then they touched Milo. "We are all real to the touch!"

The Writer continued to write, and the artist continued to paint. And every living thing in *Milo the Legend* appeared. They formed in a line. The Top Being was first in line. He held the Writer in the palm of one hand, and the artist in the palm of his other hand. They continued to write and paint.

The Holy Cow stood behind Milo. All the characters in the story lined up behind the Holy Cow. The Top Being started to dance, and everyone followed him. They danced along. It was a beautiful line dance, and then they all began to sing.

The Writer kept writing, and the artist kept painting, and everyone danced and sang across the dimension. They were all brothers and they were all full of faith, hope, love, and charity…and they would all live forever.

The Writer kept writing, and the artist kept painting.…

Yes folks, the Milo story will never end.

# Author Bio

David Waldbillig is a humble, simple man with a huge imagination.

# Artist Bio

Charity Aili Ruotsala looks at life as an adventure with God based on Psalm 139:16 and John 3:16-17.
Out of this inspiration she loves to encourage and inspire others. Her artwork, which includes customized paintings, portraits, and illustrations, is part of the adventure.
Milo the Legend has been a creative challenge of imagination with her friend, the author, David Waldbillig. Charity is married to Brian, her husband of twenty-five years. They are blessed with five children. The family are "Yoopers" hailing from Ironwood on the western edge of Michigan's Upper Peninsula. She can be reached at bcruotsala@yahoo.com.

To order additional copies of

# MILO
# The Legend

Contact Savage Press by
visiting our webpage at
www.savpress.com

or see our Savage Press
Facebook page.

Or call
218-391-3070
to place secure credit card orders.

mail@savpress.com

Discounts for bulk orders from groups or educational
organizations are available.